“Let me

Mandy’s

“Buttercup...” Unlike her harsh croak, Zane’s voice held the deep, rich tones of a man anticipating what could transpire if she’d allow him to keep this up.

He’d never know how tempted she was. “Let me go now.” She sucked in air. “We’re not doing this.”

He choked on a laugh. “Could’ve fooled me.”

“I mean it. Let me go.”

His grip loosened and he stepped back. He was breathing hard and his hand trembled as he ran his fingers through his hair, but his gaze was steady. “We need to talk about this.”

“No, we don’t.” She scooped up her hat.

He stared at her. “I just kissed you. And by the way, you kissed me back.”

“So what? You’re a good kisser.”

“*So what*? We’ve known each other since we were three and something like this has never happened before. We can’t just ignore it.”

“*I* can, and I will. What you choose to do is up to you.”

A COWBOY'S STRENGTH

THE MCGAVIN BROTHERS

Vicki Lewis Thompson

Ocean Dance Press

A COWBOY'S STRENGTH

ISBN: 978-1-946759-10-8

Ocean Dance Press LLC
PO Box 69901
Oro Valley, AZ 85737

Cover art by Kristin Bryant

Visit the author's website at
VickiLewisThompson.com

Ready for more? Check out these other titles by Vicki Lewis Thompson

The McGavin Brothers

A Cowboy's Strength
A Cowboy's Honor
A Cowboy's Return
A Cowboy's Heart
A Cowboy's Courage
A Cowboy's Christmas
A Cowboy's Kiss
A Cowboy's Luck
A Cowboy's Charm
A Cowboy's Challenge
A Cowboy's Baby
A Cowboy's Holiday
A Cowboy's Choice

The Nerd Series

Nerd in Shining Armor
The Nerd Who Loved Me
Nerd Gone Wild
Gone with the Nerd
Talk Nerdy to Me
Nerds Like It Hot
My Nerdy Valentine

Wild About You

Werewolf in Manhattan
Werewolf in the North Woods
Werewolf in Seattle
Werewolf in Denver
Werewolf in Alaska
Werewolf in Las Vegas

1

Zane McGavin made the drive back from Bozeman in high spirits. Releasing a bird of prey into the wild after a successful rehabilitation was almost better than sex. Then again, he hadn't had sex in a while so he might not be qualified to make that statement.

He'd been so busy with ranch work and the raptors in his care that he hadn't dated in months. Might even be close to a year, now. He'd reached that awkward stage of being too old for casual hookups and too young—at least in his opinion—to settle down.

Maybe if the right woman came along...

She'd have to like the idea of living in Montana, though. He was rooted in this place and he...damn, there was some idiot changing a tire right next to the road. They could get run over.

Passing carefully, he drove onto the shoulder several yards in front of the vehicle. His truck's tires ground through slush and gravel that might cause trouble for a little sedan like that one. Maybe the driver had been afraid of getting stuck. At least the car was bright red, which made it stand out.

Zane tucked his gloves in the pocket of his sheepskin jacket before climbing out. When he turned to face the disabled vehicle, he discovered the driver standing in front of the car. The belted wool coat, long hair and girly city boots told him he'd come to the aid of a lady in distress. She held a tire iron in one hand and a phone in the other as she watched him approach. Most folks around here were law-abiding, but she might not know that.

"Ma'am, I'm here to help." He held up both hands, palms out. "If you don't want me to come any closer, I'll stay put. But please call a garage to come out and change that tire for you. If you don't have a number to call, I can give you one. It's mighty dangerous for you to be working right next to the road like that."

She went very still. "Zane?"

"Yes, ma'am, that's my name, but I don't believe I..." Then it hit him. Her hair was cut different and her coat and boots weren't the style she used to wear. But he knew that voice and now that he'd moved a little closer, he knew that face, too. He'd been looking at it off and on between the ages of three and seventeen, although she hadn't been a part of his life for years. Ten, to be exact.

Maybe she'd lost her country smarts while living in the big city. "Mandy Fielding, are you fixing to get yourself killed?"

"I was afraid I'd get stuck if I pulled off any more."

"Then why not call roadside assistance?" Thinking some stranger had been risking life and limb by the side of the road had been bad enough.

Discovering Mandy had put herself in that position was making him crazy.

"Takes too long. My plane was late and Mom started her vacation this afternoon so she could be home when I arrived. This should've saved time."

"How long have you been at this?"

She made a face. "A while. The lug nuts are on super tight."

"Probably some mechanic in Bozeman got over-zealous with the power equipment." Thank God he'd happened along. Gradually the fact registered that he was standing here having a conversation with Mandy after ten years.

Their last face-to-face hadn't been great, near as he could remember. He must have ticked her off pretty bad since she hadn't tried to contact him any of the times she'd come to visit her mom over the years. She hadn't changed a whole lot since he'd last seen her, though—same hazel eyes that could look green or gold depending on her mood, same shiny, caramel colored hair. She didn't seem much older, just more sophisticated.

He'd missed her, but that was neither here nor there. She'd obviously come home to help sort through stuff since her mom was selling the house and property that bordered Wild Creek Ranch. Contacting him wouldn't have been part of the plan on this visit, either. He took a deep breath. "I'll get started on that tire."

"Zane, I don't expect you to change it for me."

"Why not?"

"Because I—look, I was rude when you invited me and Mom to the graduation party. I never apologized."

He blinked in surprise. "What?"

"I was a real jerk, especially after how long we'd been friends. Let me call roadside assistance. I'm sure you have plenty of other things to do this afternoon besides mess with my tire."

Amazing. She was guilt-ridden about some ten-year-old argument that was only a fuzzy memory to him. "I seriously doubt you were the jerk in that situation. More likely it was me."

"No, I was. I turned you down flat. Things were awful and I made them worse."

"If you say so. I honestly can't remember much about that conversation." The breeze tugged at his hat and he grabbed the brim to keep it on. "Here's an idea. Let's call it even and I'll change your tire so you can get to your mom's faster." He gave her a smile. "How about that?"

* * *

Mandy had to laugh at herself. Fate had sent her a knight in shining armor and she was doing her best to send him riding off again. "Okay. Thanks, Zane." She handed him the tire iron. "I appreciate it."

"You're most welcome." He walked around the right side of the car to the open trunk and laid the tire iron inside.

"Won't you need that?"

"Eventually. First I'm gonna move your car."

"Do you think that's a good idea?"

"Better'n getting either of us killed by a distracted driver. Besides, I'll use the truck to pull it out if I screw up." He picked up the jack and the spare tire she'd hauled out and put those in the trunk, too. "I see you only have a donut."

"Yep. It'll get me to Mom's and I'll have George fix the flat."

"George is retired." Zane closed the trunk. "But the business is operating and they still call it George's Garage."

"That's comforting."

"It's one of the things I like about Eagles Nest." He came back around the car to where she was standing. "Folks try to keep things familiar if possible." He said it with pride.

"You're right." She'd always suspected he considered her decision to live back East as a kind of defection.

"Okay, let's take a gander at what I'm heading for." Walking along the far edge of the shoulder, he kicked at the slush with the toe of his boot.

Now she knew she was in Montana. Nobody in New York City said *take a gander*.

"Should be okay." He glanced at her. "You'd better stand by my truck so I know where you are."

"Or I could stand in front of you, give directions and holler if you're heading for trouble." Just like that, she'd slipped into country talk, too. She never said *holler* except when she came back here.

He grinned at her. "Like you did with the ATV that time?"

"I see you don't have any trouble remembering that."

"Rolling backwards into Wild Creek tends to make a lasting impression on me."

"I got confused. I forgot that I was facing the opposite way from you and my right was your left. I'm older and wiser, now."

"Okay. I trust you." He shoehorned himself into the rental and moved the seat back to accommodate his six-foot-three frame.

She hadn't thought of that adventure in years. They'd been barely thirteen and if his mom had found out they'd nearly destroyed the ranch's ATV they would've been forbidden to ride it for months. Sweating bullets, they'd shoved and dragged that machine out of the creek and up the embankment. Except for a couple of new scratches, it had been fine.

Zane started the car and put down the windows. "Ideally I'd like to end up right behind my truck. That way we have two vehicles on the side of the road so oncoming traffic can spot us easier."

"Makes sense." She walked around to the front of the car. "Let 'er rip!"

The sedan's wheels spun at first, but finally the tread dug into the damp surface and Zane edged the car slowly toward the right side of the shoulder while she called out directions. She was extra careful not to mix up her left and right and by the time they finished the maneuver, he'd bought another four feet of distance from the road without getting the little red car stuck.

He rolled up the windows and climbed out. "Good job, Buttercup."

"Thanks." His use of her old nickname caught her by surprise. She couldn't remember when he'd started calling her that, but he'd hardly ever used Mandy unless he was mad at her. After their icky conversation about the graduation party she'd never expected to hear the name Buttercup again.

"I have a couple of flares in my truck." He tugged on the brim of his Stetson. "Might as well put those out, too."

"While you're doing that I'll call my mom. She's probably worried."

"You can sit in the truck. It'd be quieter."

"Thanks." She started toward the passenger side but he got there first and opened the door. She noticed the logo before he handed her in. "So what's *Raptors Rise* all about?"

"Raptor rehabilitation. I could have just called it that, but giving the project a cool name appealed to me."

"You're doing that, now?"

"On the side." He leaned against the open door. "Mom gave me permission to use ranch property and the lumberyard donated supplies to build the aviary. Oh, and you remember Kurt? He was in our class."

"I do. Serious kid."

"Super serious. He's a vet, now. He took a few extra courses in ornithology so he can work with the injured raptors, pro bono. I couldn't do this without the support I've had."

Now she understood why a large pet carrier was strapped into the bed of his truck. "So that project we used to talk about—you made it happen."

"It's a small operation, but yeah, that's how I spend my time when I'm not leading trail rides or mucking out stalls. I'm on my way home from a release."

"Of what?"

"A female golden."

"Very cool." Although the bald eagle was the national bird, she was partial to goldens. So many called this area home.

"It was great. The guy who found her in February helped with the release. Seeing her take flight was—" He broke off. "I could talk about this all day and we need to get moving. See you in a few." He closed the door.

Mandy removed her gloves so she could use her phone. Zane sure was enthusiastic about his raptor program. He'd made quite a picture leaning against the door of the truck in his sheepskin coat and brown Stetson with snow-capped mountains forming a backdrop behind him. His intense blue eyes became even more compelling when he was into something. She envied him that passionate commitment. She hadn't been that excited about a project in a long time.

Her mom answered on the first ring, which probably meant she'd started pacing. "What's up, sweetie?"

"The rental got a flat. Zane happened along and he's going to change it for me."

"Well, that's lucky."

"I know. I'm sort of glad it happened. Gave me a chance to connect with him and apologize for that whole graduation party debacle. I thought he might be holding a grudge but he's not."

"I wouldn't expect him to. He's not the type."

"And I knew that, but...anyway, do you know he's rehabilitating birds of prey?"

"Sure do. I went over there to see his setup. He's moved into that old log cabin up the hill from the ranch house and he built an aviary next to it. He's really dedicated to the cause."

"I'm not surprised." Mandy respected that about the guy. When he took on a task, he gave it all he had. "Anyway, thanks to Zane, I'll see you soon."

"Sounds good. Listen, if I know that boy, he'll follow you home to make sure you get here okay. Invite him in for coffee, if he has time."

"I'll ask him."

"Tell him I have cookies."

"I will. 'Bye, Mom. Love you."

"Love you, too, sweetie."

Mandy disconnected. Naturally her mother would have the inside scoop on Zane's activities. Her mom and the McGavins had been rural neighbors and close friends for years. Eeyore, Mandy's sad-eyed gray gelding who was now technically her mom's horse, was stabled at Wild Creek Ranch. Her mom would have had plenty of chances to check out Zane's project.

Mandy didn't want to leave town without seeing it, either. As kids, she and Zane had been fascinated by the birds of prey living in the mountains that surrounded Eagles Nest. Zane had vowed that someday he'd create a haven for those who'd been injured and she'd volunteered to be his partner.

Slipping her phone into her coat pocket, she climbed down from his truck and started back toward the rental car. He'd lit the flares and was hunkered down next to the left rear tire struggling to loosen the lug nuts. He was cussing, too, which gave her some satisfaction. If even Zane was having trouble, those things must be welded on.

When he laid the tire iron on the ground and got to his feet, she wondered if he'd given up. Instead he took off his jacket, draped it over the fender and went back to work.

The impact was like Superman ripping open his shirt. Until this moment, Mandy hadn't thought Zane had changed much in ten years. How wrong she'd been. Under his jacket he wore a snug white t-shirt, and oh, dear God, did he wear it well. The soft cotton lovingly revealed muscles that flexed and bulged as he forcefully attacked the lug nuts. She stood there transfixed and watched him twist them off.

After he unscrewed the last one, he stood, wiped his forehead with his arm and glanced her way. "Got 'em."

She snapped out of her daze and walked toward him. "Good job! What can I do to help?"

"Just hang onto these for me." He handed her the lug nuts. Then he peered at her. "Are you okay?"

"Sure am. Why?"

"You have that look you used to get when you were coming down with something. You're flushed and your eyes are really bright."

"Not coming down with something, I promise." She focused on his face because looking at his superhero pecs was likely to keep that flush going strong.

"Good. You get cranky when you're sick."

"No, I don't."

"So it wasn't you who dumped over the Monopoly board?"

"I only did that once."

"True." He flashed her a smile. "The other times it was Sorry."

His smile scrambled her brain and robbed her of a comeback. She'd seen it a million times but it had never made her speechless before. By the time she'd recovered, he'd retrieved the jack and the spare.

"I don't trust this little donut, so I'll follow you home to make sure you get there all right."

She cleared her throat. "Mom said you would. If you have time, she'd like you to come in for coffee and cookies."

"Sounds great. I'd love to."

"Good." After he went back to work, she loosened the scarf around her neck to let in some cool air. How ironic that her old buddy Zane had turned into the hottest guy she'd met in ages. It was probably a very good thing she was flying back to New York in a week.

2

Zane kept an eye on the red car's rear wheels as he followed Mandy back to Eagles Nest. He needed to focus in case anything went wrong, but it was a challenge to keep his mind on tires. Dealing with her had stirred him up.

She'd crossed his mind a few times over the years, but for the most part he'd managed to forget her. That would likely change now that he'd seen that she was...yeah, she was beautiful. He hadn't allowed himself to think that in high school because it had seemed wrong to lust after a girl who had been his best friend for a lot of years.

But their long separation had cancelled that friendship, in a way. It was almost like he was meeting her for the first time, except he'd maintained contact with her mom so he wasn't totally out of the loop. He'd heard she had a good job working for a fashion designer in New York.

That alone should tell him that interest in her was pointless. She'd transplanted herself there ten years ago and her mom said she loved the East Coast. Didn't matter if his pulse rate shot up when he looked at her. Her life was in a whole other part of the country.

Eagles Nest, the town they were currently driving through, was exactly what he wanted—small community, friendly people, incredible scenery. He wouldn't trade living in this part of the world for anything.

She'd set him back on his heels, but he'd get over it. She wouldn't be here for very long if she stuck to her pattern. A few days and she'd be flying home to New York. Then he could push her out of his mind again and all would be well.

She stopped at George's Garage to drop off the tire and he waited in the parking lot. Eagle's Nest had one major street, which someone lacking in originality had labeled Main Street. Any business of importance had a storefront there, including George's. Zane watched until she climbed back into the red car and then they were off to her mom's place.

He turned down the familiar dirt road. How many more times would he take this route now that Aunt Jo was selling? She wasn't technically his aunt, but that's what he'd called her since he was a little kid. In the years since then he'd discovered that you didn't have to be blood kin to feel related to somebody. Thanks to Aunt Jo living right down the road from Wild Creek Ranch, he had two moms.

Luckily she was only moving into town, a mere ten miles away, so she'd continue to stable her horse with the McGavins. Although Zane would see her about as much as before, it wouldn't be the same. Having somebody else own what he considered a second home would be weird.

He hoped whoever bought it wouldn't renovate because the house was perfect the way it was. Dark brown shingles and a forest green pitched roof blended in with the woods that surrounded the building on three sides. The interior was paneled in knotty pine. After spending hours there as a kid, he associated knotty pine with playing games and eating cookies.

In the summer months, the back deck was great for watching whatever wild critters wandered by. That happened a lot because the area was chock full of elk and deer, not to mention eagles, hawks and owls.

He'd miss sitting out on the deck this summer. If Aunt Jo put it on the market soon as she'd planned, it'd likely be sold before June. It was chilly out there now but he might suggest they spend an evening on her deck while they still could. She had a metal fire pit that would keep them warm.

The house came into sight through the velvet green of tall pines. He tried to imagine someone else living there and couldn't. But Aunt Jo was tired of maintaining it and that was valid.

Since her divorce she'd learned her way around a toolbox and Zane had helped whenever she'd run into a problem she couldn't handle. Because he'd served as her handyman, he had a sense of ownership about the place. But she was an independent lady who worried about imposing on him even though he'd been more than willing.

She came running out of the house without her coat when they drove up. Zane stayed in his truck for a few seconds to let Mandy and her mom have a moment. Aunt Jo missed her daughter a hell of a lot.

Seeing them together, laughing and hugging, no one would doubt they were mother and daughter. They were about the same height and both slender and fit. Zane remembered when Aunt Jo's hair was the same color as Mandy's, but she'd decided to let it go gray and she wore it super short because she didn't like messing with it.

Once the two women stopped hugging, Zane left his truck so he could help with Mandy's suitcase. Aunt Jo fussed over him and showered him with thanks for keeping Mandy safe. He couldn't take credit for a random rescue but Aunt Jo was determined to reward him in some way. Apparently, furniture was an appropriate gift.

"You need to take that sofa." She gestured to it as they walked through the front door and into the living room. "You've always liked it and you need one for your cabin."

He smiled at her. "Thanks, but don't go giving away your sofa. You might need it in your new place." The house smelled great. Her condo in town would, too, if she kept up her baking habit.

"I think that sofa's too big for the condo. Besides, I have a strong urge to get rid of everything and start fresh with new stuff. I'll have the money once I sell this house."

"That's the spirit, Mom." Mandy chimed in with enthusiasm. "New beginnings."

While Zane wouldn't mind having the sofa, he didn't want Aunt Jo giving up every stick of furniture in this house. The dining table and chairs had sat in front of the picture window ever since he could remember. He hoped she would keep them.

He offered to take Mandy's suitcase to her room but she wouldn't hear of it so he left the suitcase in the hall. They hooked their coats on the coat tree beside the door and he hung his hat there, too. At home, he tended to leave it on. It was a ranch thing.

Aunt Jo brought out the coffee and his favorite cookies, chocolate chip. But this time she'd baked them for Mandy, who was also partial to that kind. He didn't care who she'd baked them for. After wrestling with those lug nuts, he was hungry.

They settled at the table with Aunt Jo on the end and Zane and Mandy flanking her. Zane waited for one of the women to start in on the cookies.

Instead Mandy ignored them and turned to her mom, her expression animated. "Now I can finally tell you my fabulous idea!"

"What's that, sweetie?"

"Well." Mandy paused dramatically. "We've talked about you coming for a longer visit once the house sells."

"Absolutely. We'll celebrate." Aunt Jo picked up a cookie.

Zane picked up two.

Mandy took none. Whatever was on her mind must occupy all of it if she wasn't eating cookies. "So I've been thinking, why just visit?

Since you're leaving this house, why not move back East and live with me?"

Zane damn near choked on his cookie. A quick swallow of coffee saved him.

"Live in New York?" Aunt Jo stared at her daughter.

"Exactly! You can't fully appreciate the city with short visits. Even a week is not enough. But if you lived there we could explore at our leisure. The Metropolitan Museum of Art alone would take—"

"Mandy, slow down. Let me get my bearings. You're talking about a major change, here. I know the city has attractions galore, but—"

"And even though you've been there several times, you haven't even scratched the surface!"

"I hope you're not suggesting I should retire, because I—"

"Heavens, no. You're too young to retire."

"And I need the money. Even if I didn't, I like working."

"Gotcha covered, Mom. Considering all the banks there and the contacts I've made over the years, you'd have a job in no time."

Zane couldn't believe the words coming out of Mandy's mouth. Aunt Jo had seniority at the Eagles Nest bank and she was beloved by customers and co-workers alike. Surely she wouldn't give that up to start over in some huge establishment in the heart of a big city where her daughter was the only person she knew.

"Even if the job's not an issue," Aunt Jo said, "I've already made a deposit on the condo."

That should put a lid on it. Zane was relieved. Aunt Jo wasn't fixing to leave Montana, especially not to live in one of the biggest cities in the world.

But Mandy didn't seem the least discouraged by news of the condo deposit. "I'm sure you can get it back. You're too savvy about money to give someone a nonrefundable deposit. Mom, think about the fun we could have." Her face glowed with excitement. "There's so much to do there. We'd have a blast."

"I'm sure we would, sweetie." Aunt Jo reached over and gave her daughter's arm a squeeze. "I just need some time to think about it."

"That's why I wanted to tell you right away, so we can talk it through while I'm here." Mandy turned to Zane. "Can't you just see the two of us kicking up our heels in the Big Apple?"

If she was asking for his support for this crazy idea she wouldn't get it, but he didn't want to come out with a negative comment, either. "It's quite a concept, all right."

Aunt Jo sent him a look. "Sure is."

Mandy appeared to take Zane's remark as a sign of approval. "It's a great concept and this is the perfect time to do it now that the house is going up for sale."

"Mm." Zane drank coffee and ate cookies while Mandy raved on about the benefits of a move to New York. She talked about plays they would see and concerts they'd attend while her mother smiled and said very little.

Eventually Mandy paused for breath and looked across the table at him. "Pretty cool, huh?"

"Like a said, quite a concept."

"I know! I have a friend who might be able to sublet his two-bedroom apartment for a reasonable price. My lease is up next month, which is perfect timing. Oh, and I have frequent flier miles up the wazoo." She turned to her mother. "Think of it—Paris, London, Venice—the opportunities are endless."

"Sure sounds like it."

Zane couldn't get a bead on Aunt Jo's mindset. She'd mentioned the job and the deposit as if she wanted to put an end to this nonsense. Now he wasn't so sure. Maybe with those barriers removed she was considering the move. She hadn't traveled other than her trips to New York, and living with her daughter might make them both very happy. He didn't think she'd like a big city as a steady diet, but maybe she would.

"We could head south, too," Mandy said. "I've never been on an Amazon River cruise, and we—" She paused as a phone played Frank Sinatra's *New York, New York.* "That's mine. I should get it. My friend said he'd call if he got all the details worked out on the lease." She left the table and grabbed her phone from the purse she'd left on the sofa. "I'll take it in my bedroom."

After she'd dashed down the hall, Zane glanced at Aunt Jo. "A lot to absorb, huh?"

She grimaced. "You said it."

"You don't want to move?" That cheered him up considerably.

She lowered her voice. "I can't imagine living in New York, but I can't say that yet. I want to dig into this a little more and find out what's behind this brainstorm of hers. She caught me by surprise."

"Then she's never mentioned the possibility before?"

"Never. She's gone out of her way to demonstrate how happy she is and how much she loves the place, but she's never hinted that—oops, here she comes." Aunt Jo smiled at him. "So the golden release went well?"

"Fantastic." He gave her a quick overview but he could tell Mandy had info she was eager to share so he cut the story short.

The minute he did, she delivered her news. ""We can sublet the apartment! You'll love it, Mom."

Zane couldn't picture Aunt Jo moving into an apartment. She'd lived in this house a long time. But Mandy might not have taken that into consideration, or else she'd decided that the excitement of being with her in the big city outweighed everything.

But it wasn't his place to butt in, at least not yet. If he stayed much longer his opinion on the matter was liable to come out, so he pushed his chair away from the table. "I should probably head on back to the ranch and help Mom feed. Thanks for the coffee and cookies, Aunt Jo."

"Thank you for changing Mandy's tire." Aunt Jo stood.

"Yes, thank you so much." Mandy gave him a big smile as she and her mom walked him to the front door. "If you hadn't come along, I might still be out there trying to get those stupid lug nuts loose."

He shuddered to think about what could have happened to her. "Glad I was in the vicinity." He put on his coat and hat. "Let me know if there's anything else I can do while you're here." *Like help you get your head on straight.*

"Actually, there is. I'd love to see your raptor setup whenever you have time."

Now that was more like the Mandy he used to know, someone fascinated by Montana wildlife and eager to learn more. "You bet." Because tomorrow was a weekday, he didn't have any trail rides going out and no one had a riding lesson, either. "Would tomorrow morning work?"

Mandy glanced at her mother. "Did you have anything planned for us in the morning?"

"Nothing specific. If you go over there, I'll see if I can get in for a haircut in the morning. Nicole was sick last week or I would have done it then."

Zane laughed. "You don't need a haircut, Aunt Jo." It was their running joke because he wore his hair longer than hers.

"Yes, I do. Look at this." She tugged at the back of her hair. "I hate it when it brushes my collar."

Mandy glanced at him. "Looks like I need to let Mom head to the salon before she turns into her version of Rapunzel. What time should I be at the ranch?"

"I'm usually finished at the barn around ten."

"Perfect. I'll have time to pick up the tire and be at the ranch a little after that. Will your mom be around?"

"She'll make a point of it if I tell her you're coming over. I'll meet you at the house." He hesitated. "I don't know if you want to consider riding up to the lookout, but I spotted two eggs in one of the nests the other day."

"Yeah?" Her eyes took on the excited sparkle that made them look more green than gold. "I would *love* to see that."

"Then I'll saddle Eeyore for you." Things were on the upswing. The lookout used to be one of their favorite places to escape their chores and talk about stuff. Between now and then he'd figure out a diplomatic way to tell her that Aunt Jo would be miserable in New York.

3

After Zane left, Mandy glanced at her mother. "He really is a great guy."

"You don't have to tell me." Her mom gathered up the mugs and the empty cookie plate. "I've always been a fan of that boy. I love all of the McGavin brothers, but since Zane and Ryker were over more than the younger ones, I'm partial to those two."

"Is Ryker still in the Air Force?" Mandy followed her mom into the kitchen.

"Not for long. He's coming out in August. Kendra's counting the days."

"I'll bet. It'll be good to see her tomorrow." The chance meeting with Zane had given her a graceful way to reconnect with the woman who'd been like a second mom. She dumped out the coffee grounds and rinsed out the pot. "If I'm going to goof off for a good part of tomorrow, maybe I should get started on that box you wanted me to sort through."

"It's in your room and it's stuffed to the brim. In fact, let me get a second box so you can put whatever you want to keep in that."

"Make it a small box. Apartment living has taught me to pare down. I used to be quite the packrat."

"Do tell." Her mother grinned. "Can I watch? It'll do my heart good to see a reformed packrat at work."

"I guarantee I'll be pitching nearly all of it."

By the time her mom returned with a smaller box, Mandy had emptied the big one into a pile on the floor. This job would be easier if she moved quickly and didn't pause to let memories swamp her.

She didn't dread the bad memories as much as the good ones. As a kid and a preteen, she'd been oblivious to any strain in her parents' marriage. She'd lived the privileged life of an only child of doting parents. In her early teens, an undercurrent of tension in the house had made her uneasy. Her mom and dad had started fighting openly during her junior year.

She hadn't saved much from that year or the next, when the word got out that her dad's affair with his secretary had resulted in a pregnancy. Her mom had filed for divorce and Mandy's senior year had been buried under family drama. Collecting souvenirs hadn't been a priority.

But stuff from the earlier years could set off little bombs of misery if she didn't go through them fast. She tucked the Ouija board and the Magic 8 ball back in the box without looking at them. Old t-shirts imprinted with favorite cartoon characters went right in, along with friendship bracelets and action figures and a pair of jeans she'd decorated with iron-on designs.

"You're doing well." Her mom sat on the bed. "At this rate you'll be done in no time."

"That's the idea." She found a hair clip that the McGavin twins had given her one Christmas and set that aside. It was small and she might wear it sometimes. "What's going on with Bryce and Trevor?"

"They're both in Texas working on a big cattle ranch. The owner had a beer at the Guzzling Grizzly one night about two weeks ago when Bryce was tending bar and Trevor was waiting tables. He hired them both on the spot. Kendra says they're having the time of their lives down there."

"Huh." They'd been scrawny teenagers but judging from the way Zane had filled out they probably weren't scrawny anymore. "And Cody?"

"Wrangling greenhorns at a dude ranch. I forget the name but it's up near Glacier National Park."

"I have a vivid memory of him as an adorable toddler. That kid charmed everybody. Never met a stranger."

"He's still like that."

"Then he's perfect for a dude ranch." Mandy dropped several teen romances into the box along with beaded purses she and her friends had made one year. Then she picked up the only Breyer horse she'd saved out of the collection she used to have.

This one had been a palomino originally. She'd painted it gray with a black mane and tail to match Eeyore, the gelding her parents had given her when she'd turned twelve. It wasn't the greatest paint job in the world, which was one reason she'd kept the statue. The others had been in good condition and would likely have ended up on some kid's shelf, but this one might have gone into a landfill and she hadn't wanted that to happen.

She glanced up at her mom, who was watching her. "Is Eeyore doing okay?"

"Very well for twenty-four. I ride him as often as I can, and Kendra gives me a discount on the boarding fee because they've started using him as a trail horse. He's perfect for inexperienced riders."

"Thank you for taking him on." She'd avoided talking about Eeyore whenever she'd come home. If she'd mentioned him she would have been obliged to go visit him and she hadn't been ready to face the McGavins. "Do you think he'll remember me?"

"Probably. Have you ridden at all since the last time you were on him?"

"A few times with friends in Central Park." She made a face. "Not enough to get used to an English saddle, though."

"I've never tried one but I sure like your saddle. Fits me perfectly. We obviously have the same butt."

"Yeah, we do." Mandy smiled. "I'm glad you're able to use it. That saddle wasn't cheap and I doubt I appreciated how much money you had to shell out for boarding and vet bills, either."

"Hey, sweetie, if you're feeling guilty about Eeyore, let it go. Thanks to him, I got over my fear of horses."

"Yes, but you could have done that without owning one."

"But since I do, I ride him quite a bit."

"Really?"

"Yep. Kendra and I go out together, especially in the summer when it stays light for so long. We ride after I get off work and then have dinner together."

"Sounds nice." Her mom wouldn't be able to do that anymore if she moved to New York, but those frequent flier miles could get her mom back here for visits with her best friend.

After studying the horse for a moment, Mandy handed it to her mom. "Put him in the second box, please. I'm taking him with me. That might be all I want, which means I can tuck him in my carryon." She sorted through what was still on the floor and put everything in the box except an empty picture frame with her graduation year in sequins along the bottom edge.

"I couldn't remember what that frame was all about," her mom said.

"It's from my senior prom. It was the table favor."

"Oh! That explains why the picture's gone. As I recall you had a fight with your date and Zane brought you home."

"There was more to it than that."

"There was?" Her mother's forehead wrinkled as if trying to fill in the blanks.

She wouldn't be able to, though, because during that time their mother-daughter bond had been weak and confidences had been few. "Zane and his date came out of the gym after the prom was over and discovered my date had me backed up against his car while he attempted to maul me."

Her mom covered her mouth in dismay.

"So Zane pulled him off and decked him."

"Oh, sweetie. I had no idea."

"Because I didn't tell you."

"That was a horrible time, just horrible. Your dad and I were fighting, you and I weren't talking..." She twisted her hands together. "And then that creep spoiled your prom. Thank God for Zane."

"He was my hero that night. It's why I saved the picture frame." She gave it to her mother. "I'll take that back with me, too."

"As you should. And just think, he was your hero again today."

"Yeah, he sure was." Eliminating him from her life had weighed on her, but now that they'd reconnected, she was a hundred times lighter. "Is he seeing anybody?"

"I don't think he is. There was someone, but they broke up months ago."

"Anyone I know?"

"She wasn't from here and she's since moved. I can't remember her name. Kendra could give you more info."

"It isn't important. I was just curious."

"Well, since we're on the subject, anybody special in your life these days?"

Mandy chuckled. "Oh, yeah, I forgot to tell you. I'm in love with a guy named Guido. He and his pet boa constrictor will be living with us in New York. It totally slipped my mind until you asked just now."

"Okay, smarty pants. Let me ask it a different way. Would you tell me if some idiot recently stomped all over your heart?"

"Sure I would." She peered at her mother. "Why are you asking?"

"I just wondered if...well, it's just that this idea of me moving back there is so unexpected."

"Mom, give me a little credit. I wouldn't ask you to move across the country to help me through a breakup. I haven't dated anybody seriously since Anthony and I split."

"He wasn't right for you."

"Nope." She paused. "I know it seems that this idea came out of the blue, but my reasoning is simple. It's silly for us to live so far apart when we get along so well. You said today that you're ready for a fresh start, so why not go all out?"

Her mom gazed at her. "You'll need to give me time to consider all the angles, sweetie. As you well know, it's not in my nature to be impulsive."

"I do know that. It's one of the things I love about you." She gave her mother a fond glance. "But the more you consider it, the more you'll see what a great adventure it'll be for both of us."

* * *

As Zane drove down the dirt road to Wild Creek Ranch, he waved to newlyweds Greg and Libby heading out for their evening ride at a brisk trot. Not long ago Libby had never ridden a horse and now she looked like a pro.

Watching a novice become a seasoned rider was gratifying. He'd been thrilled when Aunt Jo had made the transition from someone who feared horses to someone who rode every chance she had. That was another thing wrong with Mandy's idea. Aunt Jo was comfortable riding here. Take her back East where the saddles were different and the horses were an unknown quantity and she could lose some of her hard-won confidence.

He was a little later than he'd meant to be and he wasn't surprised to see his mom in the barn with a wheelbarrow full of hay flakes. She hadn't heard him come in because she was singing along with an eighties tune playing on her phone. He smiled when she added a couple of dance steps to "Girls Just Want to Have Fun."

When he caught her in an unguarded moment like this, she looked way too young to be the mother of five adult sons. But then she'd had them early—Ryker and Zane before she'd turned nineteen and the twins a little over a year later.

A weather-related car accident had taken out both of her parents not long afterward. These days she freely admitted that having Cody had been a way to bring happiness back into her life. But Cody had been less than a year old when their dad had died, leaving her with five boys to raise and a ranch to run.

Many people would have crumbled under that weight, but his mom had grit and the challenge had brought out the fighter in her. Her dark hair had a few strands of silver mixed in, but she was as vibrant as ever.

He walked toward the wheelbarrow and sucked in the sweet aroma of hay. "Hey, Mom."

She spun around mid-lyric and grinned. "Hey, son. That eagle release must've taken longer than you expected."

"It wasn't the release that held me up. I stopped to help somebody change a tire. You'll never guess who."

"George. For a guy who used to sell tires, he has an embarrassing number of flats."

"Good guess, but not this time. Mandy Fielding."

Her eyes widened. "No kidding! Jo told me she was coming back this week but I lost track of the day." One of the horses whinnied and she laughed. "Okay, Winston, we're on it!" She glanced at Zane. "Guess we'd better keep moving before they mutiny."

"Yep." He grabbed the bundled hay and carried it into a stall. He worked one side of the barn and she worked the other. With eighteen horses to feed it was a two-person job.

He delivered the hay and patted Jake, a handsome bay with a smooth gait he'd inherited from his Tennessee Walking Horse daddy. Great trail horse.

"So how long's it been since you've seen Mandy?" his mother called out.

He carried another flake into an empty stall, one that would soon be occupied when Greg and Libby brought their horses in from the trail. "Almost ten years. How about you?"

"The same. I kept thinking she'd stop by on one of her trips home, but I guess she hasn't had time."

"Probably not." Zane didn't want her to think Mandy had deliberately stayed away, although she had. He deposited hay in the next stall, which was also empty. "She'll be here a week helping Aunt Jo pack up."

"That's what Jo said."

"But she wants to see the raptors so she's coming over around ten tomorrow."

"She is? Then she'd better stop and see her Aunt Kendra, or she'll be in big trouble."

"She will. I told her to meet me at the house. We're also taking Eeyore and Jake up to the lookout to check on the eggs."

"Just like old times." Her voice echoed a little in the barn's rafters. "I can't wait to see her again. How is she?"

Gorgeous. "A little skinnier, I think."

"Jo doesn't think she's eating right. I keep hearing about the fabulous food in New York but I wonder if people besides tourists have time to eat it."

"Maybe not." He gave a sweet-tempered roan named Strawberry his evening meal. "But there is something you probably should know before she gets here. She's pushing for Aunt Jo to pull up stakes and come live with her in New York."

"What?"

He stepped into the aisle.

His mom stood on the other side of the wheelbarrow, hands on her hips and blue eyes shooting fire. "That's the craziest damn thing I've ever heard. Jo would hate living in New York. What's Mandy thinking?"

She didn't swear often, which indicated how strongly she must feel about this. He did, too. This would be bad for Aunt Jo, but also for the McGavins. Aunt Jo was considered a member of the family and Mandy was trying to pluck her out from under their noses. "Mandy talked about all the things they could do together."

His mom blew out an exasperated breath. "But Jo's gone back there at least a half-dozen times, maybe more. She's seen the sights."

"Mandy says she's barely scratched the surface."

"Maybe so, but she hardly needs a degree in all things New York. She's happy here. She's finally coming into her own after twelve years of being divorced from that slime-ball Robert—" She clapped a hand over her mouth.

He laughed. "It's okay. I've heard him called worse."

"Probably by me. He was horrible to Jo, but treating Mandy that way was unforgivable."

"How did he treat her?"

"When he got his new family he cut off communication."

Zane gritted his teeth. "You never told me that."

"You weren't in touch with her anymore so there was no reason to. Please don't mention it to her."

"I won't. But thanks for telling me. It's good to know."

"Jo was ready to kill him with her bare hands. He's lucky he doesn't live here anymore. It would be bad for his health."

"No kidding." His heart ached for Mandy.

"I suppose her dad's rejection could have something to do with this gonzo plan, but it happened years ago." She heaved a sigh. "Relocating there would be rough on Jo, but she loves that girl and she might do it if Mandy puts the pressure on. It's a terrible idea but I won't say anything. They need to work it out."

Zane hated to think how Aunt Jo leaving would affect his mom. If she moved into town things wouldn't change much. If she moved across the country, they would. His mom wanted to let them work it out, but he couldn't just stand by and say nothing. When a train was barreling toward a broken trestle, he felt the need to shout a warning.

He still wasn't sure what form that warning would take, but he had until tomorrow to figure it out. Luckily he and his mom would be video chatting with Ryker tonight. Ryker wouldn't like this any better than he did.

4

Several hours later Zane and his mom were set up for the video chat. Ryker missed the ranch, so they always set up the laptop so he'd have a view of something he loved. When it was warm, they sat in rockers on the front porch and when it was cold, they switched to the living room with a fire going.

The fireplace arrangement was trickier. Including the fire without sitting in pools of sweat took engineering, but they'd worked out a system with chairs in the foreground and the fireplace in the background. They put the laptop on a box on top of a card table.

They'd been doing this routine for years now, and Zane still wasn't used to thinking of his brother on the other side of the world facing danger every day. Ryker had been determined to follow in their late dad's footsteps and join the Air Force, but Zane wanted him home, not flying the unfriendly skies and risking his life. If talking to Ryker made his stomach churn, his mom had to be even worse off.

But no one would ever know it. Every time they started a video chat and Ryker's smiling face popped up on the screen, she always smiled right back and asked how he was, her voice filled with warmth and optimism. She followed the same routine again tonight.

"Fine, Mom," he said, as usual. Ryker was always fine. He never complained or discussed whatever bad stuff was going down. Despite that, the weariness in his gaze spoke of those things even if his words were upbeat.

He'd also taken to wearing a battered old cowboy hat during their chats. Some buddies in his outfit had found it at a flea market and had presented it to him because he'd earned the nickname Cowboy somewhere along the line. The hat covered his buzz cut and made him look less like a soldier and more like the Ryker Zane loved.

"So what's up?" Ryker always asked right away because he didn't want to talk about his life and was obviously hungry for news from home.

Zane described the golden eagle release and Ryker's ever-present smile broadened. "Well done, bro. That makes my day knowing she's back out there where she belongs."

"And driving home he came to Mandy's rescue," their mom said. "She had a flat on the way in from the airport."

"I'll be damned." He looked at Zane. "Did you two have a semi-normal conversation after all this time?"

"We did. She's coming over tomorrow to see the raptors and ride to the lookout."

Ryker nodded. "That's excellent news. Tell her hello for me. How long will she be in town?"

"A week. She's helping Aunt Jo pack up the house."

"It's on the market?"

Their mom shook her head. "It will be soon."

"I hope we like whoever buys it." Ryker repositioned his worn hat. "Hard to think of strangers living in that place."

"No worries, son. Jo promised she'd engineer a meeting between any prospective buyers and me before she signed the papers. I have veto power."

"That's great, Mom." Ryker lounged back in his chair. "Aunt Jo's always looking out for us McGavins. It won't be too bad having her living in town. I'll bet she'd let me sleep on her sofa if I decide to have an extra beer at the Guzzling Grizzly."

"About that." She cleared her throat. "Mandy's trying to convince Jo to move to New York."

Ryker sat bolt upright. "What the hell?"

"It's true." Zane was glad his mom had brought up the subject because if she hadn't, he would have, even if it was potentially bad news. "I was there when she presented the plan to Aunt Jo."

"How did Aunt Jo react?"

"Startled, but she didn't totally reject it, either. Then Mandy left the room to take a call and Aunt Jo admitted she wasn't crazy about the idea."

"No surprise, there. She'd hate living in a big city."

"That's what I said." Zane was more convinced than ever after hearing Ryker's opinion.

"Listen, bro. If you and Mandy are buddy-buddy again, you need to talk her out of this."

"Nope, nope." Their mom waved her hands at the screen. "We're Switzerland, totally neutral. It's a complicated dynamic and Jo's the one who has to decide."

Ryker leaned closer to the screen. "Sorry, that won't work. You're a mom. You know how moms are. If they think their kid desperately needs something even if it requires great sacrifice on their part, they'll do it, especially if it's an only child."

Another face appeared over Ryker's shoulder. "I'd listen to him, ma'am. Cowboy's wise beyond his years."

Ryker snorted. "Get lost, Badger."

"Just wanted to put in my two cents. Sounds like a knotty problem. I wish y'all luck with it. 'Bye-bye, Cowboy's mom and Cowboy's brother. Cool about the eagle release, by the way."

"Don't mind Badger," Ryker said. "He was transferred to our squadron three weeks ago and dropping in on everybody else's video chats is his thing. Hell of a pilot, but a royal pain in the butt."

Zane laughed. "Sounds like my kind of guy."

"Glad to hear it, because I told him he could bring his sorry ass for a visit when he gets out."

"He's more than welcome," their mom said. "But despite his opinion of your great wisdom, Mandy and Jo should work this out on their own without comments from the peanut gallery." She gave Zane a pointed glance.

"Mom, I love you to pieces," Ryker said, "but I completely disagree with you. I'd talk to Mandy myself except a video chat wouldn't be as effective as ol' Zane making the case in person."

"Neither one of you should talk to her. You need to leave it alone."

"Like I said, I love you but you're mistaken, Mom. Aunt Jo needs backup on this deal. Hey, I'm getting the signal to sign off. Give my love to Cody, Bryce and Trevor."

"Will do." She got up and walked closer to the screen. "Stay safe, son."

"Always. See you both soon." The screen went blank.

Zane walked over and put his arm around his mom, who had reached out to touch the blank screen. "He'll make it home."

"I know." She swallowed. "And the day he does will be the best day *ever*."

* * *

A mixture of eagerness and anxiety gave Mandy the jitters as she left the main road and drove the narrow dirt lane toward Wild Creek Ranch. It was as if she'd been here yesterday but also a lifetime ago since she'd parked beside the house and walked around to the front porch.

The one-story log house looked basically the same, but the pitched roof's original shingles had been replaced by dark green galvanized tin. She used to play in the attic under that slanted roof with Zane and Ryker and they'd all loved huddling up there during a rain. The tin roof would make it even more fun, although those two big guys wouldn't fit too well in the cramped space.

The fancy cast iron knocker in the shape of a lariat hadn't been on the carved front door the last time she'd stood in front of it, either, and the boot scraper was new. She used it to clean her boots, or rather, her mom's boots. Her entire riding outfit was thanks to her mother. They'd fit into the same size since Mandy turned fifteen, but she hadn't worn her mom's clothes until today.

As she reached for the knocker, the door opened. Aunt Kendra gave a whoop and grabbed Mandy into a tight hug. "I'm *so* glad to see you! I thought I heard your car, so I decided to come and..." She held Mandy away from her and looked her up and down. "You look *exactly* like your mother did at twenty-seven. Same hair, same eyes, same smile. To think she was younger than you are now when I first met her."

"Hard to believe." Mandy was a little shaky, but Aunt Kendra's enthusiasm helped.

"Come on in and take off your coat. Zane texted me that he has a few more things to take care of down at the barn."

Mandy left her coat and hat on a coat tree that was just like her mom's and walked into a living room filled with reminders of her childhood. She'd spent hours here racing around like a maniac playing chase with the boys, making tents with blankets and watching cartoons on TV. She wondered if Aunt Kendra still had the train set they'd played with endlessly.

"Have a seat." Aunt Kendra waved her to a cushy chair and perched on the sofa. "I think Zane's dawdling on purpose. He knows how much I wanted to see you and find out how you've been. How's the job?"

"It's good." Mandy gave her standard answer. "I've always loved fashion and working for an innovative company is fun." The thrill wasn't there anymore, but she hoped to get it back.

"I'll bet it is fun." Kendra slipped off her shoes before curling her feet under her. "Your mom said your boss is great."

"She is. She takes me with her to some of the shows, which is fabulous experience for whatever I want to do in the future." She had no idea what that was, but surely she'd figure it out soon. "You look terrific, Aunt Kendra."

"Thanks." She combed her dark hair back from her face. Silver strands made it appear professionally frosted, although more likely it was natural. "I put on makeup this morning because you were coming. How silly is that? But you're from the big city, now, and so I..." She waved her hand in the air. "I spruced up."

"I've always thought you were beautiful."

She blushed. "Wow, thanks again. Your mom's the natural beauty around here. Not many women can wear a short haircut like hers and still be stunning."

"She's beautiful in a different way, but you're both my role models."

Aunt Kendra waved her hands in front of her flushed face. "You're totally embarrassing me, but thank you."

"Listen, before Zane shows up, let me apologize for not coming to see you when I visited Mom."

"Hey, don't worry about it." She gazed at Mandy with affection. "You're here, now. Let's start there."

She exhaled with relief. "I see where Zane gets it."

"Gets what?"

"His ability to forgive and forget."

Aunt Kendra smiled. "I learned a long time ago that life's short. It was a very hard lesson but it stuck with me. I tried to pass it on to my boys."

"Zane has it down pat." She hesitated. As a kid, she'd accepted that Aunt Kendra's husband and her parents had all died. She hadn't thought to question it, although somewhere along the way she'd heard about the car accident. But she knew nothing about Aunt Kendra's husband's death. "Forgive me if this is a terrible subject, but how did your husband die? I've never known, but if you'd rather not—"

"It's fine. It took me a while, but I've come to terms with it. Ian died instantly from a brain aneurism at twenty-four."

Mandy flinched. "How awful."

"Yep. And ironic. After surviving three years of aerial combat missions, he ended up dying of something that would never have occurred to either of us at that age."

"That's so sad, especially so soon after losing your parents."

"I won't pretend it was easy, but I'm still a very lucky woman. My parents willed me the ranch and I can't imagine living anywhere else. Ian gave me five amazing sons, and I'm grateful for that every day. They've kept me going during times I wanted to give up."

Mandy gazed at her in admiration. "What a wonderful attitude."

"I give a lot of credit to my women friends, especially your mom. She has a knack for knowing just what to say or do."

"Yes, she does." Mandy loved hearing Aunt Kendra praise her mother. The move to New York would separate those two good friends, but maybe Aunt Kendra would fly back there for a visit. Having both Aunt Kendra and her mother in the city would be incredible.

She started to mention the potential move, but the sound of a door opening in the back of the house signaled that Zane was on his way.

Aunt Kendra called out to him. "We're in here!"

"Figured!" Seconds later he walked into the living room bringing with him the scent of pine and enough masculine energy to set Mandy's blood humming.

She left her chair because seeing him made her restless and eager to move. "Hey, Zane."

He touched the brim of his Stetson in greeting. "Hey, Mandy. Get the flat taken care of?"

"I did." She loved the way cowboys said hello. Two fingers touching the brim of a Stetson was sexy as hell, but she hadn't admitted that until a couple of seconds ago. A man in a tux could be dashing, but she'd take a cowboy in a Stetson any day.

Aunt Kendra stood and gave her another hug. "Zane said you two were riding up to the lookout."

"That's the plan."

"You're welcome to stay for lunch afterward if you have time."

"That sounds great, but Mom should be home from her hair appointment about then and we're supposed to clean out the garage today."

"I don't envy you. I hope I never move. Cleaning out the attic would do me in. Anyway, I'd love to see you again before you go back."

"Let's plan on it." Mandy noticed that Zane had grabbed her jacket off the coat rack and was holding it for her. She thanked him as she slipped it on. He'd done that for her a bunch of times in the past because he had cowboy manners, but today the gesture felt like a caress.

She was probably imagining things. Settling her hat securely on her head, she waved goodbye to Aunt Kendra and left with Zane. As they started up the hill to the cabin where he stayed, she asked how many birds he was caring for.

"Seven. Used to be eight before the release yesterday. I have another female golden and she should be released in a week or so. She's more than ready to go. Her mate keeps coming by to check on her."

"You're sure it's her mate?"

"I'd bet on it."

"I never thought of what happens with a mated pair if one gets injured."

"Probably depends on the circumstances, but he was nearby when I found her tangled in baling twine."

"Was anyone with you?"

"No, and that made it a challenge. I wondered if her mate would attack me but he didn't. I took off my coat and managed to wrap it around her."

"This coat?" She looked at the sheepskin jacket he was wearing, the same one he'd had on the day before.

"Yep. Had to have it professionally cleaned and a couple of places mended, but that's okay. I brought her back here and Kyle doctored her claw. Her mate followed me and that lovesick bird's been hanging around ever since."

"Aw." What an image—Zane riding home in bitter cold wearing only his t-shirt with the eagle wrapped in his warm jacket.

"In fact, that's him, right up in that pine tree, about halfway to the top." He paused to point into the branches. "See him?"

"No."

"To the left a little more." He took her by the shoulders and repositioned her. "Now look straight up. See him?"

"I don't...oh, wait, now I do." She acted as if having Zane take hold of her like that was nothing special. Once upon a time it wouldn't have been. But that was then and this was now. He smelled delicious, a combination of evergreen and aftershave. "He's big."

"She's bigger." He let go of her and stepped away.

"Right, she would be." She glanced at him. "I remember the day we found out that the females are larger than the males. You weren't happy."

He grinned. "I got over it. Come on. Let's go see the gang." He led the way to a wooden structure a short distance from the small cabin that had been the original home of the couple who'd built the ranch.

She remembered the cabin fondly. She and the McGavin boys had been allowed to play in it years ago, but it was perfect for Zane now that he had the raptors to care for. The aviary reminded her of a giant chicken coop, although she'd never seen a circular one before. Supported by what looked like fence posts, it stood about four feet off the ground and was at least eight feet tall. Chicken wire divided it into pie-shaped sections and a pointed tin roof sheltered the cages.

Because it was in the shade of several large pines, Mandy couldn't see into the enclosures very well and she didn't want to startle the birds by getting too close. "Am I likely to scare them?"

"Not if you go slow. I think the shade helps them feel safer because they're more camouflaged. The bird you're heading toward is hard to see, anyway. He's not very big."

She crept forward and peered into the enclosure. At first she saw only a gnarled branch, but then something moved and two golden eyes stared right at her. Her breath caught. "Oh, my gosh. You have a pygmy owl."

"Yes, ma'am." He came to stand behind her.

Her body responded to the heat of his and she fought the urge to move back and snuggle against his chest. A girlfriend would, but she wasn't his girlfriend. "Hard to think of an adorable little bird like that as a raptor."

"But he is, all seven inches of him. Rescue folks don't name the critters they will be releasing because then we might stop thinking of them as wild animals. But I gave in and called him Socrates."

"Cute." What would she do if Zane put his arms around her and pulled her close? Not that he would. "Where did he come from?"

"Some kids found him huddled in the snow out on the playground. He'd been shot in the wing with a pellet gun. Naturally they wanted to keep him, but their parents convinced them he'd be better off here until he's well enough to be released."

"Hey, Socrates." Mandy leaned closer to the wire. "You're precious."

The little owl blinked at her.

"Zane, I'm in love."

"Yeah, join the club. Aunt Jo and Mom adore him, too."

She stepped back, careful not to bump into Zane. "It must be hard to let them go."

"Sure. I get attached to them while they're here, but they're wild. They don't want to stay.

When I remind myself of that, it's easy to release them. It's what they want."

"You're right." Mandy gave the little owl one last look before moving away. "Who else do we have?"

"I'll introduce you around, but none of the others have names."

"I can see why that's a good idea. I'm already attached to Socrates." She followed him as he pointed out the golden female with the injured claw, a male golden who'd been shot in the chest, and a bald eagle who had also become tangled in baling twine.

"Baling twine is a real problem for eagles," he said. "They find it lying around, use it for their nests and get snared by it. Those three are my eagle population. The other three are hawks." He continued to move around the structure. "I ended up modifying the enclosure for these two red-tailed ones because they wanted to be together."

She smiled. "How could you tell?"

"Just watched them in their separate cages. Seemed obvious after a while. They're young so they might be brothers who got in the way of someone with a pellet gun."

"You say that so calmly. It makes me furious to think a person would do that."

Zane shrugged. "Some folks were never taught to respect nature."

"Have you ever caught someone shooting at them?"

"Once. Heard them up by the lookout and followed the sound. Fortunately, he was a bad shot and hadn't hit anything yet."

"What happened?"

His eyes took on a steely glint. "The guy wasn't real cooperative when I first told him his behavior was unacceptable, but I think he finally got the idea that keeping it up wouldn't work out well for him. Besides, he'd have to buy a new gun."

"Why's that?"

"It's amazing how flimsy they are. One good whack against a boulder and they're useless."

"Gee, what a shame."

"Yeah." He held her gaze and the space between them shimmered with energy. Then he drew in a quick breath and turned toward the aviary. "This last one is a Cooper's hawk. Kyle found her by the road pretty banged up. He thinks she was after prey and crashed into a windshield. She's coming along, though."

"She's lucky. All of them are. Do you have a website, a way for people to donate to the cause?"

"Not yet." He rubbed the back of his neck. "Fact is I should build another aviary like this one before I spread the word or I'm liable to get more birds than I can handle. Besides feeding them and checking their progress, I exercise the ones who can fly by taking them to the flight cage as often as possible."

"Where's that?"

"In that little meadow near the creek. I'd show you but we don't have time to go there and it's not very interesting. Just a wood and wire enclosure where they can keep in shape."

"I wish I had time to help you while I'm here." She wished it more than she'd expected to. "Unfortunately, clearing out Mom's place will take most of the week."

"I understand."

"But your setup is great, Zane. Really great."

"Thank you." His gaze warmed. "Glad you like it."

"Who wouldn't?" For the first time in her life she considered kissing him. Imagining what that might feel like gave her the shivers and she looked away. "Guess we should get the horses and head on up to the lookout. I want to make sure I'm home by the time Mom's finished with her hair appointment."

He nodded. "Right. Let's go." He started down the hill.

His voice had sounded funny, though. She was super aware of him as they walked side-by-side toward the stable. What if he'd considered kissing her?

5

Zane wasn't pleased with himself. Last night's video chat had established what needed to be done regarding Mandy's plan to move Aunt Jo to New York. Ryker had delegated him to convince Mandy it was a bad idea.

He'd been pumped to do it until he'd seen her today in her cowgirl duds looking so happy to be visiting his birds and riding up to the lookout with him. He didn't want to spoil everything with a discussion that she might not like all that much.

On the other hand, her plan was a huge mistake, so wouldn't a good friend point that out and try to get her to reconsider? In years past he'd thought he could talk to her about anything. If he could recreate the easy familiarity they'd had before her parents' drama had screwed it up, she might give some weight to what he said regarding her mom and New York. Or she might pitch a fit and never want to see him again.

On top of that issue, he had another one. When he gazed into her eyes, he wanted to kiss her. Now there was a truly bad idea. He'd also wished he could gather her close and offer comfort for the rotten way her dad had behaved.

But he wasn't supposed to mention that so he had no excuse to give her a hug, either.

This attraction was doomed so he might as well quit daydreaming about what could never be. He could so easily lose track of his goal—convincing Mandy that her mom needed to stay in Eagles Nest. If he failed, Aunt Jo and the McGavins would suffer.

He, Ryker and their mom would take the biggest hit. Zane didn't want to think about how Ryker would react if Aunt Jo was gone by the time he came home. Those video chats had provided a clear image of the world Ryker expected to be waiting for him and Aunt Jo was part of the picture. She was a second mother to him, too. She'd always been there, if not as a replacement for their dad, at least another parental type who doled out love, advice, and the occasional reprimand.

But that wasn't the important point to make with Mandy. He didn't want to end up in a tug-of-war where they argued about who should get to live in the same zip code as Aunt Jo. Mandy had a lock on that because of biology. Instead Zane would emphasize how the move would negatively impact the woman they all loved.

At least he would if he could focus on the issue at hand instead of drinking in the sight of Mandy decked out in boots, jeans, a denim jacket and a hat that made her look like she had in the old days. Back then, he'd been used to seeing her dressed that way. The effect was different now and gave him inappropriate and counterproductive ideas.

He'd saddled Eeyore and Jake in advance and had left them tied to the hitching post. They made quite a pair. Jake stood tall and proud, mahogany coat glistening and head up. Eeyore had adopted the pose that had earned him his name. Head drooping and ears at half-mast, he appeared old and feeble, barely able to stagger out of the yard.

He put on the same performance for the trail riders. Zane always had to assure them that it was an act and Eeyore wasn't about to keel over.

Zane glanced at Mandy. "See, your horse hasn't changed a bit."

She sniffled and her eyes watered.

"Are you okay?"

She nodded, but tears rolled down her cheeks.

Damn, she was crying. "Mandy, he's fine. He's doing what he always does, making a bid for sympathy."

"I know." She swiped the tears away. "I'm not worried that he's on his last legs. Mom told me he was healthy." She gulped. "I've missed him, that's all."

"Oh." He pulled a bandanna out of his back pocket and handed it to her.

"Thanks." She stopped and blew her nose.

He waited while she got herself together. When it came to women, he struggled with the crying part, which could signal so many different things. A flood of tears could mean they were happy, sad, frustrated, scared or furious. Take your pick. He doubted Mandy was frustrated, scared or furious, so that left sad and happy. "I didn't mean to make you sad. Maybe I should have saddled a different horse."

"Absolutely not!" She tucked the bandanna in her jacket pocket before she hurried over to Eeyore and began loving on him.

The touching sight of Mandy hugging her horse didn't help Zane focus on the problem at hand. It should, because Eeyore was Aunt Jo's horse now and she was nuts about that silly animal. Riding Eeyore was another thing she'd sacrifice by moving to New York.

But instead of concentrating on that, he was captured by the reunion of a woman with the horse she'd adored as a girl. Eeyore behaved as if he remembered her. Despite his perpetually sad eyes, he looked sort of happy. He bumped his nose against Mandy's chest like he used to when she was riding him all the time.

Zane got a little emotional when he saw that. Eeyore never did it with him, his mom or Aunt Jo. Now he sympathized with the old gray horse, too. Eeyore clearly preferred Mandy to the rest of the humans who cared for him, but he was out of luck. Mandy didn't live here and wasn't likely to.

Eventually the love fest between Mandy and Eeyore let up enough that she noticed Jake. "Now there's a handsome fellow. I don't remember him." Then she hugged Eeyore's neck. "Don't worry, sweetheart. You'll always be my favorite."

"This is Jake." Zane smoothed a hand down the white blaze on the gelding's nose. "We got him about a year after you left. He's a fantastic horse."

"Looks like he would be with those long legs." She untied Eeyore and swung into the saddle. "I'm so out of practice. Thank goodness we're only going to the lookout and back."

"Yes, ma'am, quick trip." He untied Jake and mounted up. "Want to lead or follow?"

She gazed up at him. "As if you have to ask. I already feel like I'm Poncho to your Cisco so I for sure don't want to bring up the rear."

"You remember the way?"

"Maybe not, but I guarantee Eeyore does." She started out of the yard toward a well-defined trail.

Zane followed, curious to see what would happen. Eeyore was used to taking the main path through a clearing and into the trees. If Mandy gave him his head, he'd likely go that route and miss the turnoff where a narrow trail wound up a rocky slope to the lookout.

He waited for Mandy to ride past the turnoff, but at the last minute she neck-reined Eeyore to the left and started up the lookout trail. She hadn't made that turn for years, but she remembered. She looked at home in the saddle, too.

He got a charge out of watching her. Despite spending all those years in the big city, she hadn't forgotten her country roots. If she had, they wouldn't have much chance of reaching a mutual understanding about her mom. He was counting on her country roots because transplanting Aunt Jo would be painful for everyone, including

Mandy. If she succeeded in getting her mother to leave and it didn't work out, that could cause bad feelings for years to come.

For now, though, he was rocketed back in time as he followed Mandy up the steep incline. Dislodged pebbles tumbled down the slope and Eeyore groaned in protest as he always did on this part of the trip. Mandy laughed and told him not to be a baby. Her laughter said she was having fun, and that gratified him.

Until yesterday her happiness hadn't been on his conscious radar. When she'd rejected his friendship ten years ago, he'd done his best to stop caring about her happiness. He might have failed in that effort.

Judging from the way his chest tightened when she whooped and hollered going up the last, very steep part of the trail, he cared about Mandy's happiness. He wanted to see her grow and thrive in an environment that suited her. Maybe she'd found that in New York City. His mom had mentioned the innovative design company that meshed so well with Mandy's creative flair.

But if she had a fulfilling job and friends she enjoyed, would she be so excited about having her mother move back there? Not likely. She'd be content to visit her mom in Montana every so often and allow Aunt Jo to create her own ideal environment.

Mandy reached the top, dismounted and spread her arms wide. "Thank you, Zane! This is something I've missed desperately without even knowing it."

That was a promising comment. "Then I'm glad we're here." He swung down from the saddle and ground-tied Jake. The horse was so well trained that he'd stand right where Zane had left him for a good hour or two.

"It's not like New York doesn't have vistas because it certainly does. I can get a great view of the city from a rooftop bar, but what's laid out here is so much wilder and unpredictable. The cityscape doesn't change a whole lot except for the weather."

He was encouraged by everything she was saying. Maybe they'd come to a meeting of the minds, after all. "So how do you feel after that ride?"

"Fine."

"Good to hear." He pulled his binoculars out of the saddlebag and handed them to her.

"This looks like the same pair you had before." She looped the strap over her neck.

"Yes, ma'am." He'd saved up until he'd finally had enough to order them from a catalog when he was twelve. "Still work great."

"I don't know what happened to mine. Probably out in the storeroom in one of the boxes Mom and I plan to go through this afternoon."

"If you find them, don't give them away." He unstrapped an old army blanket from behind his saddle. "Those were top-of-the-line and if you don't want them anymore, I'll take them. Wouldn't hurt to have an extra pair around." He'd secured the blanket into a tight roll with two sections of twine. Normally he didn't bother bringing it but he wanted Mandy to be comfortable.

"I might as well give them to you." A breeze kept blowing strands of hair in her face. Taking off her hat, she leaned over, gathered her hair with one hand and crammed the hat on again as she stood up. "That's better. Should've done that in the first place."

"Why didn't you?" Had she wanted her hair to look pretty for him?

"Like I said, out of practice for riding. Anyway, if I locate the binoculars I'll set them aside for you. I can't think of a reason for me to keep them."

He couldn't imagine living in a place where you didn't need binoculars. If he had a second pair he'd carry one in his saddlebag all the time so he'd never be caught without a way to survey the landscape or the critters inhabiting it. "Did you bring gloves?"

"I did." She pulled them out of her pocket. "I remember how the last part goes."

"I keep thinking I should dig the rocks out a little, create more handholds so it's not such a challenge." He put on his gloves. "But I haven't done it yet. Ready?"

"You bet." She tucked the binoculars inside her jacket so they wouldn't bang around while she made the steep climb to the rock ledge.

Because she'd managed the trek so often in the past, he wasn't too worried about her, but by following he'd be in position to help if necessary. The ledge wasn't easy to access but it had several things going for it. Besides providing a view of the surrounding forest and the snow-capped Absarokas, it got sun nearly all day, which warmed the rock and melted snow quickly. In summer the rock got toasty by nine, so he usually came out early in the morning. Midday was perfect this time of year.

They were almost to the top when Mandy's foot slid on loose shale. Grabbing an outcropping for balance, she let loose with a curse.

He gazed up at her. "Need help?"

"Not sure, yet. Let me assess." She had one foot planted but the other one kept slipping wherever she tried to get purchase. "How did we used to do this in cowboy boots?"

"Lots of practice."

"Yeah, and I'm out of practice. I don't want to come crashing down on you."

"Hang on." He gave the blanket a mighty heave that sent it sailing over the lip and onto the ledge. "I'll come up and give you support so you can reposition your feet." He'd been here so often lately that he knew which rocks were stable and which ones weren't. He climbed until he could wrap an arm around her waist. "Gotcha, Buttercup."

"Thanks." She sounded a little breathless. "What now?"

"I'll hoist you up to the next handhold and reposition your feet." He'd better do it soon, too, because holding her warm body against his with her bottom pressed tight against his package was having a predictable effect. "From there you should be able to grab the ledge and pull yourself over."

"Got it."

"You'll want to get a hold on the sparkly white rock on your right and the tan one on your left. When I say *now,* let go."

"Okay."

"Now."

She let go.

He lifted her until she could reach the next handhold. "Got a good grip?"

"Yep. Just fix my feet and I'll be fine."

"Yes, ma'am." When he grasped her calves to position her boots on solid rock, he felt firm muscle under the denim. "Can you see where I put your feet?"

"Yes."

"There's another good spot about fifteen inches above that. It's a small ledge. See it?"

"I do."

"I'll stay right here while you get the rest of the way up. If you need a boost, let me know."

"I can make it."

He braced himself so he'd be ready in case she slipped while hauling herself up and over. He pretty much had to observe the process, but he shouldn't be enjoying the view of her ass quite so much. Once they were both up there he ought to rid his mind of that arousing sight. Yeah, sure.

By the time he joined her she'd taken off her gloves and was working on the twine that he'd used to tie up the blanket.

He stuffed his gloves in his pocket and helped her, which meant being close enough to catch the scent of her perfume. She was breathing fast from the difficult climb. He was breathing fast for a different reason, but she didn't have to know that. They folded the blanket in half and laid it in the exact spot where they used to sit as kids.

Then she held up the twine. "Is this the stuff the eagles scavenge that causes so much trouble?"

"That's it." He took in a lungful of pure mountain air. There. He was gradually calming down. "I either recycle it or reuse it but I never leave it lying around."

"Then I'll put it in my pocket until we tie up the blanket again." She pulled out the binoculars and put the lens protectors in her pocket, too. "Which nest has the eggs in it?"

"That one." He pointed to a tall pine.

She raised the binoculars and focused on the tree. "Yep, there's the nest. Wow, is it the same one that was there before?"

"Same one. They come back every year."

"But it's huge!"

"They keep adding to it. Can you see the eggs, yet?"

"No. The female's sitting in it so I can't...oh, wait, she just stood up. I see the eggs! Two of them!" Still looking through the binoculars, she took a step forward.

"Hey." He put his hand on her shoulder. "Remember the rule."

"It's okay. I know where the edge is."

"Mandy, please sit on the blanket. You can see fine from there."

She lowered the binoculars. "All right. But I wasn't the one who almost fell off that time." She walked to the blanket and sat on it cross-legged before looking through the binoculars again.

"I might be dead if you hadn't yanked me back by my belt."

"Then you definitely need to sit on the blanket when you're using these. There's no way I could yank you back now that you've bulked up."

"What do you mean, bulked up? I haven't changed that much."

She laughed. "Have you looked in a mirror lately? I was going to ask you if you've been lifting weights to get that muscle definition."

"Just lifting hay bales." He thought she might be paying him a compliment about the muscles, though, and that was nice.

"Then you must lift a lot of them."

"I'm mostly the one available to do it."

"Now she's sitting on the eggs again." Mandy pulled the strap over her head and handed him the binoculars. "Want to look?"

"Sure. Thanks." He focused on the huge nest that had been in the tree for years. "I pulled twine out of there three weeks ago. It didn't come from our ranch, but seeing it told me I have more community education to do."

"Run that by me again."

"I haven't spread the word enough. I should probably print up some fliers about the danger of twine and post them around town. That would—"

"No, the part about you taking it out of the nest. How'd you get up there, fly?"

"I bought some spiked boots like the lumberjacks use and got somebody to teach me how they work."

"You *climbed up?* That nest has to be forty feet in the air!"

He lowered the binoculars and found her staring at him, her eyes wide. "I was careful. I used that strap thing the lumberjacks cinch around themselves as they go up."

"There's nothing careful about climbing forty feet in the air. Talk about getting yourself killed! Does your mom know you did that?"

"Yes, and she wasn't happy about it, but somebody had to get that damned twine. I couldn't bring a crane and a bucket in there. The trees are too close together."

"I suppose, but...why didn't you hire a lumberjack?"

She had him, there. His mom had asked the same thing. "Because I wanted to do it. I wanted to see what it was like to have an eagle's eye view."

"The truth comes out. You're insane."

He grinned. "Mandy, it was awesome. Those spiked boots work great, and being at the top of the tree, cleaning out the nest and knowing I was the only person who'd been that close to it, was a blast. I'd do it again in a heartbeat."

She shook her head in obvious disapproval. "Boys." But she was smiling when she said it, like maybe she was kind of impressed with his daredevil trick of climbing that tree.

All things considered, he might not have a better moment to bring up the subject at hand. "I know we need to get back fairly soon, but—"

"Yes, we do." She lifted her face to the warmth of the sun. "This has been nice, though.

Thanks for bringing me up here and giving me the final boost." She laughed. "Not one of my more graceful moments."

"You did fine. I doubt you do much rock-climbing in the city."

"There's a climbing wall in the gym where I work out, but no loose shale."

"Loose shale's a pain." He hesitated. "Listen, before we head down, there's something I wanted to ask you about."

"What's that?"

He gazed into her eyes as he debated the best way to start. Damn, he didn't want to start at all and risk losing the nice mood they had going, but he and Ryker had pledged themselves to give Aunt Jo backup. She needed their help to save her way of life. "I've been thinking about your mom going to New York."

"Me, too. A lot."

Maybe there was hope. "So you're reconsidering?"

"Not at all. But she has a fair amount of reluctance towards making the move. Change is hard. I get that."

He forced himself to ask the tough question and prayed she'd take it well. "Is there any possibility that she's resisting because the move isn't right for her?"

The friendly light left her gaze as the color changed from mostly green to a determined gold. "I don't think that's for you to say."

She hadn't taken it well. Now he was in for it.

6

Anger pushed Mandy to her feet. She'd been basking in the warm sensual glow of reconnecting with an old friend who was more tempting than she'd counted on. But the outing wasn't much fun anymore and she was ready to bail. "We should probably get going."

"You're upset." He stood, too.

"Disappointed, mainly. It sounds like you might have brought me up here just so you could talk to me about that."

"No, I swear I didn't. When you mentioned wanting to see the raptors that reminded me of the eggs. I thought you might like to see them."

"I did want to see them. That part was great, but the way you approached the subject of my mother felt planned." She did her best to keep from overreacting. But what had looked like a chance to renew their friendship and maybe indulge in some unrealistic romantic fantasies now appeared to have a hidden agenda.

"Only from the standpoint of not knowing if I'd have another chance to talk to you about it while you're here."

"When did you conclude that you had to talk to me about this?"

"I've been thinking about it ever since you first said something. Last night I figured out the trail ride might give us the perfect chance to discuss it."

Then he'd anticipated the conversation, perhaps rehearsed what he'd say. "I feel ambushed."

"That wasn't my intention."

"Maybe not, but it turned out to be the result."

"Listen, I get that you think this is none of my business."

"Correct." Feeling the need for protection, she folded her arms.

"But your mom's important to me, almost as important as my own mother."

Okay, so that was where he was coming from. She got it. "So you don't want her to leave, and that makes perfect sense. She's been a part of your life for a long time and you'll miss her."

"Of course I will, but this isn't about me, or my mom or my brothers. It's about Aunt Jo. She's lived here for twenty-four years. I've heard her say how much she loves her job and her customers. She—"

"She loves it because she doesn't know anything else! She deserves a chance to try a different kind of life, one she might love as much or more than this one."

"Maybe, but I've never heard her say that the big city intrigues her. Has she ever hinted that it might be fun to live there?"

"No, but why would she? She had the house, and like you, I thought she wanted to stay in it. But when she announced she was selling, that opened up all kinds of possibilities, including coming to live with me in New York."

"Mandy, think about it. She's lived in this area more than half her life and I know for a fact she loves everything about it—the people and the amazing vistas. You said yourself that Manhattan doesn't offer this kind of scenery. She'll be trading a peaceful rural environment for crowds of strangers and endless traffic noise. She'll be miserable."

"Excuse me?" She got right in his face, like she used to when they'd argued as kids. "She'll be living with her beloved daughter. I hardly think she'll be miserable!"

"Come on, Mandy. She *loves* Montana."

"She also loves *me*."

"Of course she does! But that doesn't justify trying to coop her up in a New York apartment!"

"What justifies you telling me I shouldn't?" As her anger bloomed, she moved even closer and poked her finger into his chest. "This is just like you, Zane McGavin, thinking you know what's best for everyone."

"Not everyone. But I know Aunt Jo and she—"

"She is *my mother*." She poked him twice to emphasize those two words. "You have a mother and four brothers. I have *one person* who cares about me." She jabbed her finger into his chest again. "Me and my mom, we're the only family we've got. Butt out, McGavin!" She drew back her finger to jab him again.

"Stop it!" Breathing hard, he caught her hand and yanked her against his chest. "Stop doing that."

"Why should I?" Wild and reckless emotions coursed through her as she focused on eyes darkened with hot anger. But that wasn't the only emotion there. He wanted her. "It's not like little ol' me can hurt big muscular you."

"I'm not so sure." Without warning, his arm snaked around her waist and his mouth came down on hers.

Both their hats hit the ground. At first she fought him, pushing at his massive chest and struggling to get away. But it was only a token effort. They could fight this battle with words or they could fight it this way.

It was a kiss filled with fury and frustration on both sides. His mouth was demanding, as if he could convince her to agree with him. She wasn't about to cave just because he was damned good at this kissing thing. She hurled that energy right back at him and was gratified by his moan of desperation as he delved deeper, thrusting his tongue into her mouth and pulling her tight against his aroused body.

In response, she hooked her leg around his to bring them even closer. If he thought he could subdue her with a kiss, she'd show him that she wasn't that easy to manage. He'd find out how a strong woman reacted to…to…uh-oh. He'd changed tactics. His mouth gentled on hers, sipping and tasting as if savoring every delicious moment.

No fair. He was supposed to be aggressive, not seductive. He was...ahhh...turning her slowly inside out. Soft pressure, a lazy slide of his tongue and she gradually melted against him. She tried to summon her former resistance but it was going, going, gone. Combing his fingers through her hair, he cupped the back of her head and had his way with her mouth.

Heaven. Without the battle that had raged before, kissing him was so easy, so natural. What a revelation. The man who gave the best kisses she'd ever enjoyed in all her twenty-seven years turned out to be her old buddy Zane.

They had a blanket available...an image of them rolling around naked on it brought her to her senses. She was *not*, absolutely *not* having sex with this man for a million and one reasons. If she stopped kissing him for two seconds, she'd remember what they were.

She tried pulling away, but his grip tightened as he continued his sweet assault. Yes, she could bite his tongue, but she didn't want to inflict real damage, especially to such a talented tongue. Instead she grabbed a fistful of his longish hair and tugged.

He lifted his mouth a fraction from hers. "Ow."

"Let me go." Her voice sounded like a rusty hinge.

"Buttercup..." Unlike her harsh croak, his voice held the deep, rich tones of a man anticipating what could transpire if she'd allow him to keep this up.

He'd never know how tempted she was. "Let me go now." She sucked in air. "We're not doing this."

He choked on a laugh. "Could've fooled me."

"I mean it. Let me go."

His grip loosened and he stepped back. He was breathing hard and his hand trembled as he ran his fingers through his hair, but his gaze was steady. "We need to talk about this."

"No, we don't." She scooped up her hat.

He stared at her. "I just kissed you. And by the way, you kissed me back."

"So what? You're a good kisser."

"*So what?* We've known each other since we were three and something like this has never happened before. We can't just ignore it."

"*I* can, and I will. What you choose to do is up to you." She leaned down, gathered up her hair and crammed her hat back on as she stood upright. "We should go." She picked up his hat and handed it to him.

He took it but didn't put it on. "Look, I was there. I felt you respond. You want me as much as I want you."

She wasn't about to admit to damp panties and tight nipples. He didn't have to know about either. "This episode was an aberration, like we stepped into an alternate reality for a while. We'll both be better off if we pretend it never happened."

"Who says?"

"I do!" She felt panic rising because he looked so appealing standing there all mussed and manly. "So we kissed each other. Why are you making such a big deal out of it?"

"Because it is a big deal, damn it." He took a deep breath. "At least to me." His eyes were trained on her like lasers. "I can't speak for you."

Dear God, he was sexy. But she needed to appear calm and in control even though the blood rushed through her veins, making her dizzy and disoriented. "It was just a kiss. Nothing earthshattering. We don't have to talk about it, dissect it, or worry about it. It's over."

A muscle twitched in his jaw. "You are a maddening woman." He put on his hat and tugged the brim down low. Then he made quick work of rolling up the blanket and tying it with the twine she handed him.

Wordlessly she scooped up the binoculars and tucked them inside her jacket.

"I'll go down ahead of you." He put on his gloves and picked up the rolled blanket.

"Thanks. I'd appreciate that." As shaky as she was, the climb down would be more of a challenge than the climb up. Having him there ready to catch her was reassuring, but she'd prefer that the trip down not include the kind of contact they'd had going up.

She'd had a buzz going ever since he'd wrapped his arm around her waist to help her onto the ledge. When he'd murmured *gotcha, Buttercup*, her entire body had thrilled to that tender phrase. He'd reacted to their close encounter, too, judging from the evidence that had pressed against her backside as he'd held her. Later, sitting on the blanket, knees touching as they discussed the eagles and his crazy stunt to clean out the nest, she'd been aware of his every movement, his every breath.

When he'd destroyed that tantalizing moment, he'd changed the game to something far more erotic. Anger and sexual arousal were a potent combination. She hadn't known that before.

***

Zane insisted on taking care of the horses following their silent ride back to the ranch. In years past Mandy would have argued that she should do her part. But she must have been as eager to get away from him as he was to get away from her. After giving him the binoculars and muttering a terse *thank you for the trail ride*, she made a beeline for the house, jumped in her little red car and headed out.

Zane stood and watched to make sure she was truly gone. He sure as hell didn't relish going back to the house only to find her chatting away with his mom as if nothing was wrong.

Turning to the two horses standing patiently by the hitching post, reins looped around the saddle horn, he heaved a sigh. ""At least I can depend on you two to have some common sense. You're not even ground tied, but did you consider cavorting off somewhere to cause problems? You did not. The world has enough troubles without adding more."

Jake bobbed his head up and down, making his bridle jingle. Eeyore just stared in sad-eyed agreement.

"Appreciate the support. Much as I love those raptors, they lack empathy. Take Socrates, for example. I've tried having conversations with him and he just stares at me like he doesn't give a hoot." He laughed at his own joke as he replaced their bridles with halters.

His brothers made fun of him for carrying on long conversations with the horses, but he loved doing it, especially when he had some issue to work through. Horses were good listeners. Confiding in a sympathetic audience gave him insights he might not get otherwise. Right now, though, he just needed to blow off steam. He'd done a slow boil while heading home a couple of lengths behind the source of his current frustration and he could still feel the tension in his neck and shoulders.

"That woman has me tied up in knots," he told Jake. "If I'm lucky, I won't lay eyes on her again. I used to like her, but now I hope she stays the hell away from here." He turned to Eeyore. "Although I'm sorry for your sake." He gave the gray horse a pat. "I know you're partial to her, but you need to get over it."

Eeyore groaned as if he'd expected disillusionment all along.

"My feelings, exactly." Zane took a closer look at both bridles. They could use oiling so maybe he'd add that to his list of chores for later in the day. He intended to wear himself out with chores. After unsaddling both horses, he hauled everything into the tack room and picked up the grooming tote.

Winston called out a greeting from the far end of the barn.

"Hey, Winston! Be glad that your days as a ladies' man are over, buddy. Nothing's straightforward when sex is involved."

Winston snorted in response. He was the most vocal horse of the bunch, and because he was also stocky and assertive, Ryker had named him after Winston Churchill. The taffy and white Paint always held up his end of a conversation.

"Yeah, I'm not telling you anything you don't already know."

Winston nickered in reply.

"You're right. Kissing her was definitely a mistake." He started out of the barn. ""Won't be making that one again," he called over his shoulder.

He brushed Eeyore first because age had its privileges. As he concentrated on the pressure points left by the saddle, he couldn't help thinking about the contrary woman who'd sat astride that saddle. "I was just talking to Winston. He's not impressed with my efforts so far."

Eeyore turned his head to give him a look of resignation.

"Yeah, but you think everything's a lost cause. Reasoning with Mandy didn't work out and kissing her *really* didn't work out but there's gotta be something I can do for Aunt Jo."

The gray horse gave a mighty exhale and farted.

Zane laughed. "Okay. I'll take that under advisement."

After Zane finished grooming both horses, he put them in the pasture so they could search out the few shoots of grass that had poked up in the last couple of days. Then he grabbed a quick lunch in his cabin and checked on the birds before going back to the barn to muck out stalls and oil bridles. That kind of work usually had the power to quiet his mind, which would be a special blessing today.

All the horses except Winston were out in the pasture, which provided him with plenty of empty stalls to clean. He'd kept Winston in the barn ever since the gelding had overdone it racing around the pasture during a warm day last week. The stiffness in his foreleg was almost gone but he needed to be a hundred percent before the weekend trail rides. With his showy coat and take-charge manner, Winston was a favorite.

Grabbing a wheelbarrow and a rake, Zane tackled the stalls closest to Winston. He filled and dumped a few wheelbarrow loads and worked up enough of a sweat that he took off his t-shirt and used it to mop his face.

Then he draped the shirt over Winston's stall door. "I just feel so helpless, buddy."

The Paint snorted and came over to have his nose rubbed.

"Aunt Jo's been there for me so many times over the years and now when she needs a champion, I can't come up with a single idea that will help her out."

Winston's little grunt of sympathy was so like him.

"Thanks, buddy." Zane doubted the horse understood the words, but he sure responded to the tone. "I mean, here comes Mandy with her crazy idea, when Aunt Jo is already stressed about selling the house. Who wouldn't be after living somewhere for twenty-four years? It's gotta be a hassle when she starts thinking about the listing, the showing, finding a buyer who won't be a pain in the ass for my mom..."

The horse gave a short nicker.

"Yeah, that last part might be Aunt Jo's biggest stressor." He leaned on the rake. "I know a hell of a lot of people in this town, Winston. I wonder if I could nose around and find her a good prospect. Then she wouldn't have to go through all that." He went back to cleaning stalls, pleased with the concept.

The big brainstorm didn't hit until he'd switched to oiling bridles. Why hadn't he thought of it before? Maybe he could help Aunt Jo and the raptors at the same time.

7

Zane allowed his idea to percolate as he quickly finished oiling the bridles. He wanted to boot up the computer in the office before his mom came back from her grocery run. If he found a bunch of stumbling blocks once he went online, he might ditch the whole thing without mentioning it.

She got home before he'd accomplished all he'd wanted to do, but he had enough to light a fire under him. When the front door opened, he called out to let her know he was in the office.

"Okay." She sounded cheerful. "Thought I'd make chili for dinner if you want some."

"Thanks! I'd love it." He kept checking facts and figures while she moved around in the kitchen putting things away.

Eventually she appeared in the doorway. "I saw Mandy and Jo in town. They were buying touchup paint. I'm glad they decided on that instead of repainting."

"Me, too." They wouldn't need to bother with any of it if his idea worked.

"Mandy was acting a little weird, though. I asked if she'd seen the eggs in the nest. She was enthusiastic about the eagles, but something was off about her. She didn't want to look at me."

He shrugged. "She's hard to figure sometimes."

"Actually, I think she's a little bummed because her mom isn't jumping on the New York proposition. Jo called when you two were out riding. This has thrown her for a loop."

"And you told her she and Mandy had to work it out?" Not likely.

She sighed. "That sounded great in theory, but I can't refuse to comment when my best friend's sorting out a problem."

"I know."

"You're right that she doesn't want to go. But she doesn't have a handle on why Mandy's asking her and she wants to know that before making a decision." She studied Zane. "Do you know why she's come up with this idea?"

"Not a clue."

She hesitated, as if wondering whether to continue the discussion. Then she waved her hand as if pushing the topic out of the way. "What I said last night is true, though. We're not the people who can solve this." She glanced at the computer. "Doing raptor research?"

"No, I've been checking comps to find out what the Fielding place would likely sell for."

"Jo did that a couple of months ago, but I can't remember what she found out. Why were you looking that up? Did you run into a hot prospect for her?"

"Yes, ma'am." Now that he was about to say it, his chest tightened.

"Who's that?"

"Me."

Her jaw dropped. "You? Why would you want to buy Jo's house, for God's sake?"

"As it turns out, for lots of reasons. For one thing, you'd get along with your new neighbor."

"Zane, that's not a reason to make such a major purchase." Her gaze narrowed. "What's going on?"

"Nothing complicated." Not strictly true but close enough. "I could use it for Raptors Rise."

She looked skeptical. "Why? You have plenty of space to build more aviaries if that's what you're thinking about."

"I don't really need more land, although I'm glad the Fielding property is a couple of acres. I want the house for my headquarters."

Her eyes widened. "Headquarters?"

"Exactly. I could put up a sign on the main road and another one in front of the house. I could have a small reception area in the living room and use one of the bedrooms for intake and to house severely injured birds. If I raised the funds, I could put some medical equipment in there so Kyle wouldn't have to bring his." He paused for breath. "The list goes on."

She walked over and sank into a chair in front of the computer desk. "I had no idea you had such a big dream."

"You know what? Neither did I until today when I started thinking about Aunt Jo selling that house."

"Could you even swing it?"

"I think so." He smiled. "As it turns out, I know somebody who has an impressive title at the bank and I'll bet she'd vouch for me when I apply for a loan."

"No question about that." She looked uncertain. "But your rehabilitation program sounds like a much bigger deal than I thought it would be. How much time would you need to be there?"

"Not any more than I spend at the cabin now. Part of my signage would have my cell number for info and assistance. If it's an emergency, it's a two-minute ride over on the trail." He rarely took that route as an adult but when he and Mandy had been buddies he'd kept it well worn.

"But making the operation more visible will probably cause it to grow."

"That would be great and should bring in more donations. If I need to hire someone to staff it while I'm working here, I'll probably have the money, but I might get some volunteers, too."

"So you're not thinking of cutting back on leading trail rides?"

"No, ma'am. I'll put in the same hours as always at the barn, too. I'll never give up working with horses while I can sit a saddle. The raptors are a sideline, but I feel good helping them."

His mother took a deep breath. "It's a noble cause, too. Besides, I can guarantee Jo will be thrilled with your idea. But it means she could leave that much sooner if she has a buyer for the house."

"You know I don't want her to leave at all."

"I don't either. But if Mandy makes a strong enough case, I think Jo will move to New York even if that isn't her first choice."

"Does that seem right to you?"

"What I think doesn't matter. If Mandy needs her there, she'll go."

He'd simmered down quite a bit while planning his rehabilitation headquarters, but now his irritation with Mandy returned full force. "Then Mandy should be tickled pink if I offer to buy the house right away. She can have what she wants that much faster."

His mom gave him a knowing glance. "You two had a fight when you went on your ride."

"Doesn't matter."

"No, I guess it doesn't. When're you planning to talk to Jo about buying the house?"

"I need to check a few more things and see what interest rates are these days on a thirty-year mortgage." He turned off the computer. "We should go feed, though, so I'll come back to this tonight. But to answer your question, I thought I'd ask Aunt Jo if I could go over there tomorrow sometime."

"You don't want to wait until after Mandy leaves? If you two aren't getting along, that might be better."

"She might encourage Aunt Jo to list it while she's here. There's no reason to go through all that if I'm going to buy it."

"Jo will love that part. She wasn't looking forward to having real estate agents and prospective buyers tramping through her house."

"I had a feeling." Yep, this was the right thing to do. Aunt Jo would be happy and even Mandy should be thrilled. If she wasn't thrilled, too bad.

* * *

Mandy had set aside the next morning to tackle the bathrooms and kitchen with touchup paint. Luckily all three rooms were the same shade of off-white and she'd been able to match it after finding an old paint can while cleaning out the garage. She'd hit on the painting scheme after finding out that her mom intended to spend the morning sorting through boxes of pictures and photo albums. No thanks.

She hadn't brought painting clothes so she dug out her old jeans and a slogan t-shirt from the box of giveaways. Hard to believe that she'd once thought a tee that said *Too Sexy for My Shirt* was cool or that hot pink looked good on her. But for a morning of painting, the clothes were perfect. She pinned her hair on top of her head, pulled on rubber gloves and got started.

Her mom sat in the living room with her boxes of pictures and Faith Hill on the stereo. Last time Mandy had walked through there she'd seen a wedding album lying on the sofa. Ick. Talk about a nightmare in the making.

Her mom's phone rang, followed by "Hi, Zane!"

Mandy stopped painting to eavesdrop.

"Sure, come on over."

Mandy squeezed her eyes shut and muttered a swear word.

"No, no, the timing's great. You're not interrupting a thing. Mandy's painting and I'm sorting pictures. I'll put on a pot of coffee. See you soon." Moments later her mom came into the kitchen. "In case you didn't figure it out, Zane's stopping by."

"What for?" She'd almost said *what the hell for.*

"He has an idea he wants to run by me. Didn't say what it was." She looked at Mandy. "Why is your face all scrunched up like that?"

"I think I got some paint in my eye."

"Oh! Let me—"

"That's okay." She stripped off her rubber gloves. "If you'll put the lid on the paint and stick the brush in a baggie, I'll run into the bathroom and look in the magnifying mirror." Maybe she could get away with staying there until Zane left.

Dashing into the bathroom, she took inventory of her bedraggled self. She didn't want to see Zane at all, but she certainly didn't want to see him when she looked like this—no makeup, her hair going every which way and her clothes...ugh. But if she changed her mom would read too much into it.

The hot pink t-shirt was snug, but it hadn't mattered when nobody but her mother would be around to read the slogan stretched across boobs that were quite a bit larger than they'd been at thirteen. The godawful color made her skin look flushed, or maybe it *was* flushed because she'd soon face the man she'd mistakenly kissed with great enthusiasm.

The decorated jeans were tight, too and she'd decided not to wear shoes. She was fine going barefoot around the house, but she didn't care for the idea of going barefoot in front of Zane. Never mind that he'd seen her naked feet a million times when they were kids. As that moment on the ledge had demonstrated, they weren't kids anymore.

But all she had were her fancy boots, her mom's that she'd borrowed to ride in and her red velvet slippers. No help, there. She splashed cool water on her face in hopes it would take some of the redness out. As she grabbed a towel, her mother went to the door and greeted Zane. He'd made excellent time.

"You rode Jake over here!" Her mom sounded delighted. "Mandy, guess what?" she called out. "Zane took the trail over like he used to when you were kids."

"How about that?" She had no choice but to finish drying her face and come out of the bathroom looking pleased as punch. "Hey, Zane."

"Hey, Mandy." His gaze flicked over her and he pressed his lips together as if trying not to laugh.

After seeing herself in the mirror, she couldn't blame him. Then, because karma was out to bite her on the butt this morning, Faith Hill launched into one of her biggest hits. As "This Kiss" poured from the stereo, Mandy's face began to heat.

Zane ducked his head with a muffled snort.

"Jeez, but I hate that song." She rushed over to the stereo and hit the off switch.

Her mom looked startled. "Since when? You used to love it. You knew all the words and you were glued to the TV whenever the video came on. I distinctly remember you dancing around the—"

"Sure, when I was ten. Who's ready for coffee? I'll get it." With a smile that probably looked more like a grimace, she hurried into the kitchen and snatched three mugs from the cabinet. She bobbled one and had to clutch it against her chest to keep it from hitting the floor.

"Personally, I think it's a great song." Zane's voice was slightly louder than necessary, as if he wanted it to carry into the kitchen.

"Me, too." Her mom matched his volume. "One of my favorites."

As Mandy poured the coffee, she'd bet the two of them were lifting their eyebrows and shrugging as they stared at each other in bewilderment. *Good job, Mandy. Way to play it cool, girlfriend.*

"I'm sorry." She used a tray to carry all three steaming mugs into the dining area. "It really is a great song and I did love it once, but unfortunately now it stirs up some unpleasant memories."

"That's a shame." Her mom gave her a sympathetic glance.

"I guess I'm the opposite from Mandy." Zane pulled out a chair for her mom. "That song brings up a really nice memory."

"I'm glad for you." She avoided looking at him and grabbed a chair before he could get around the table to help her. If he was referring to yesterday so he'd get a rise out of her, then he'd succeeded. If he was referring to kissing someone else in the past...yuck. She didn't want to think about that, either.

Her mom picked up her coffee and glanced over at Zane. "So what's this idea of yours?"

"It has to do with this house. I want to buy it, Aunt Jo."

Mandy gasped. This wasn't happening. Any minute she'd wake up from a bizarre nightmare. Zane couldn't buy this house. She hadn't gotten around to picturing a new owner, but she sure as hell didn't want this man buying her childhood home.

"You do?" Her mom looked taken aback. "Why?"

"To use as my headquarters for Raptors Rise. If I bought it, I could—"

"This is a *house*." Mandy's heart raced. "Not a—"

"Let him finish." Her mom put a hand on her arm and gave her a stern glance. "Go on, Zane."

Mandy listened in dismay as he described his plans for the place she'd called home. It would no longer function as a family dwelling. He'd use one of the bedrooms as an infirmary and another as an operating room. He'd been hampered by the lack of a good indoor facility for his raptors but this would solve that problem.

She had a sudden Alfred Hitchcock vision of birds in the bathroom, birds in the kitchen, birds perched on the back of the sofa…*everywhere.* She liked and respected birds, especially raptors. They were cool. But they belonged outside.

Zane continued to lay out his dream of turning this cozy home into a…a *facility.* Didn't he realize how wrong that would be?

Apparently not. He described where he'd locate the reception area and how he'd create signage out on the main road so people could find the place. The kitchen would be handy if he decided to hold a small fundraiser here and have refreshments for potential donors.

His voice grew more animated the longer he talked, while Mandy became sick to her stomach. Her mom wouldn't go for this, though. She'd put a lot of work into this place so she was probably thinking of a diplomatic way to tell Zane that he was barking up the wrong tree.

At last he finished and sat back. "What do you think?"

Her mother smiled. *Smiled.* "I think it's a fabulous idea."

Mandy stared at her in disbelief. "You do?"

"Absolutely. I'd love knowing this house would be going to someone I care about who's also making such a difference for those wild creatures."

Oh, God. She had zero power in this situation. The house belonged to her mom and her mom thought this travesty was an awesome concept. "But...but the house is set up for a family."

Her mom's gaze was serene. "That doesn't mean it couldn't be converted into something a little different. Besides, if Zane buys it, I can come back here anytime I want. I couldn't do that if a stranger takes possession."

"Well, I sure wouldn't want to come back here. It'll be totally different."

Her mom squeezed her arm. "Sweetie, that's going to happen regardless of who buys it, and I'll bet Zane can use some of the furniture so it won't be *that* different."

And the nightmare was complete. Her mom would give him the sofa and birds would perch on it. They'd sit on the backs of the dining room chairs, too, and the oak headboard in her bedroom.

"I wouldn't mind having some of the furniture, Aunt Jo," Zane said. "But I'll pay you."

"Not necessary. You're saving me time and trouble, plus a real estate commission. How soon would you like to close?"

"Whenever you're ready."

"Then Mandy and I will step it up." Her mom beamed at her. "Right?"

She felt a cry of denial working its way up her throat. But making a scene now was a bad strategy. "I hear my phone. Excuse me." She made a dash for her bedroom, closed the door and managed to cram a pillow against her mouth before collapsing face down on her bed. Then she yelled into the pillow until she ran out of breath.

Flopping to her back, she stared up at the ceiling where a decorative hook was still screwed into the plaster. She'd hung a rotating disco ball from it once upon a time. Good thing it was gone now that Zane and his birds would be moving in.

Turning her head, she looked out the window to the soft green of the pines that surrounded the house. The green and gold curtains had been part of a redecorating project she and her mom had tackled when she'd turned twelve. She'd picked out the wrought iron curtain rods on a trip to Bozeman. They'd make great bird perches, too.

Here was the bottom line—Zane couldn't have this house, and he certainly couldn't have it for the purpose he had in mind. She'd have to talk him out of buying it.

8

Zane lounged in a tattered easy chair that was one of the few pieces of furniture in the one-room log cabin. He'd hoped building a fire, drinking a beer and reading a mystery would calm his nerves and make him sleepy, but it wasn't working. Instead he kept seeing Mandy's expression as he'd described his plans for the house this morning. She hadn't just disliked the idea. She'd hated it.

Despite his vow that he didn't give a damn, her reaction bothered him. Apparently, she'd imagined a family buying the place. He didn't know why that should matter to her but that was the only conclusion he could draw.

The fire had died down to a bed of glowing embers. Although it was late, he considered adding another log and opening a second beer. Dropping the empty bottle in the recycling bin, he walked toward the refrigerator. He paused when someone rapped on his door.

Could be his mom, but he doubted it. She'd text rather than show up unannounced. When he found Mandy on his front stoop bundled up in a jacket, scarf and knit wool hat, he blinked in surprise. "What are you doing here?"

"I came to see you."

What the hell? Completely kerflummoxed, he peered past her but couldn't see her red sedan parked next to his truck. "Where's your car?"

"I walked over on the path." She held up her phone and turned on the flashlight app. "Mom's asleep and I didn't want her to hear me leave. Can I come in? It's cold."

"Um, sure, sure." He was having trouble processing this turn of events, but he could at least be more hospitable. "Want a beer?"

She walked in and unwrapped the scarf. "That would be great." She glanced around. "Guess I should have brought my own chair."

He grinned at the image of her hiking along the path lugging an armchair. "You can have that one. I'll use the stool."

"Or I could sit on the bed."

"No, please. Take the chair." He didn't want her anywhere near the bed.

But she was headed over there anyway. She peeled off her jacket and tossed it down, quickly followed by her scarf, hat and gloves. "Nice quilt. Looks warm."

"It's wool. Won it at a church raffle." He handed her an open beer and gestured toward his easy chair. "Have a seat."

"No, really, that's your chair. I can—"

"Mandy, please sit in the damn chair, okay?"

"Okay, okay." She settled into it and wiggled her butt to get comfortable. "Thanks for warming it up."

She was being nice. He wondered what she was up to, but decided not to be that direct. "You're welcome." He grabbed the three-legged stool from beside the hearth. It was left over from his childhood and he had a fondness for the workmanship. He hadn't sat on it for years, so he lowered himself with care.

"Is that the same stool that you—"

"Yep."

She smiled. "You look cute sitting on it. Like a grownup at a kid's tea party."

"Exactly what I was going for." He gazed at her. She wore the fancy boots he'd seen that first day when he'd changed her tire, her decorated jeans from this morning, and a yellow sweater. Her favorite color. He'd forgotten that until now. She'd worn yellow a lot and maybe that's why he started calling her Buttercup.

"Bet you wonder why I hiked over here."

"The question crossed my mind. Was it fun?"

"Spooky fun. The moon's almost full and I love the way it peeks in and out of the trees as you walk along."

"That is pretty cool." How did she survive in a big city without those encounters with nature? He'd go crazy.

She took a quick swig of her beer before focusing on him. In this light her eyes looked more gold than green. "But coming here wasn't just an excuse to take a nighttime walk in the woods."

"I figured."

"I'm here to ask you very nicely not to buy the house."

"I was afraid of that."

She huffed out a breath. "You only came up with this idea today, so how committed can you be?"

"I'm committed to the raptors. Expanding the program will increase my ability to help them and buying the house would be a way to do it. Simple as that."

"But couldn't you add on to the cabin and accomplish the same thing?"

He put his beer on the floor so he could concentrate on the discussion now that they were down to brass tacks. "In theory, but the cabin's historic and I'd rather not destroy the original look of it."

"Okay, then another building nearby."

"A bigger operation might interfere with ranch business, which is our bread and butter. This is and always will be a sideline."

"Exactly! If you expand like you were talking about today, it could take over your life. You wouldn't have time to lead trail rides or do your share around the barn. You'd—"

"I'd bring in help with the raptor operation before I'd let that happen. I'll hire somebody if the donations justify that or put out the word that I need volunteers."

Her jaw tightened. "I still think it would impact your work at the ranch."

That's not for you to say. But he wouldn't throw her words in her face. "I might have to juggle my obligations, but the result would be worth it. I've unconsciously controlled the scope because of the physical limitations I have here. I could make a real impact on the problem by setting up a headquarters practically next door. That excites me."

Having her sitting only a few feet away excited him, too, but in a very different way. He'd take care not to let on.

"Wouldn't it be better if you rented a storefront in town? That would be way more visible."

He shook his head. "It wouldn't be bird-focused. The raptors need to be in the same location as the headquarters so people can see the birds and understand the urgency. But these are wild creatures. I won't take birds to town and turn them into a window display."

"But you will put them on display at the house, in a sense."

"Not any more than they are now. I won't allow noisy crowds of people out by the aviaries."

"Will you let them fly free in the house?"

He stared at her. "Are you kidding?"

"No, I'm not."

"These are wild creatures, not pets. I'd never turn them loose in the house." He studied her. "Is that why you were so upset this morning? You thought the house would become an aviary?"

She shrugged. "The way you were talking, it seemed possible."

"That wouldn't be safe for the birds or the people who come to visit. The atmosphere will be controlled and low-key."

"Yeah, with big signs everywhere."

"They won't be huge signs. You make it sound like I'm setting up a theme park. It's a non-profit with an environmentally friendly concept. The last thing I want is to make it look like a roadside attraction for tourists."

She drank more beer and scowled at him. "You'd probably decide to pave the road leading into the property, though."

"That's pricey, but I'll definitely keep it graded more than it is now. I'd rather not have a potential donor break an axel on the way there."

"The road's not *that* bad."

"It is that bad. I followed you home the other day because you were driving a little car that could get lost in one of those potholes. The road hasn't been a priority for your mom, but it would be for me."

"Obviously." She folded her arms and crossed her legs. Her body language screamed resistance.

"Mandy, what's the problem? I thought you were in favor of the raptor program."

"I am. I truly am. I just...I don't want you to buy the house and use it for that. I don't want my bedroom turned into an infirmary or an operating room."

"What difference does it make what happens in your bedroom?" He almost laughed because that was funny, but she might not think so. "Once your mom sells the house, whether to me or somebody else, the new owner can do whatever they want, including tear it down and start over."

Her eyes widened. "Nobody would do that!"

"I hope not because it's a great house. I love the dining area with a view of the deck. Hell, I love the knotty pine paneling. I wouldn't dream of changing that, but someone else might rip it out."

"That would be awful." She took a shaky breath. "But...Zane, please don't buy the house."

"Why not? I thought you wanted your mom to live with you in New York ASAP."

"I do! We'll have a terrific time there, too." The jut of her chin said it all.

"Okay." He approached the subject with caution. She was very smart and would have made valedictorian except she lost her concentration their senior year. He'd given her credit for being logical, too. "If I buy the house now, your mom will have the funds to make that move sooner."

Her chin lifted a notch higher. "She'll have the money to finance a move after she gets back the down payment on the condo."

"Technically she will, but—"

"There's no rush to find a buyer. She might get a better price during the summer when it's warmer."

"But surely she'd feel better about leaving if the house is sold."

"Not necessarily." She took another gulp of her beer. "If you think of yourself as a white knight riding in to make her life easier, then—"

"I don't. This is supposed to be a mutually beneficial arrangement."

"You might see it that way, but Mom and I have been taking our time cleaning out all the stuff that's accumulated over the years, and then you show up ready to close on the house immediately and start moving medical equipment in. That's too...too abrupt."

"Like I said, I thought she'd like not having to go through the listing process, the open houses, the last-minute requests to show the place."

"Or she can head off to New York with me and leave the real estate agent to handle all that. Instead you're yanking the house out from under her before she's ready."

He held onto his temper with difficulty. She really was a maddening woman. "I'm not *yanking* anything. Aunt Jo can set her own timetable. I'm not trying to push her into this but I thought having a buyer, one she knows and trusts, would take some of the pressure off."

"It might if you weren't planning to make all these changes and transform it into something completely different." Her voice rose. "Have you considered all the loving care she's put into that house?"

"I know she has."

Her hand trembled as she set her empty beer bottle on the floor. "She might be too polite to say so, but I'll bet she's cringing at the idea of her pretty little guest room becoming a surgical ward for injured birds."

"Then I'd better have another talk with her. I got the impression she'd be proud to know that her former house would be a center for promoting the health and safety of these raptors. Are you saying she doesn't feel that way?"

She propelled herself out of the chair and loomed over him, her eyes shooting sparks. "I'm saying...Don't. Buy. The. House."

Struggling to stay calm, he stood, too. They were inches apart. He absorbed the heat and frustration she was giving off but had no idea what to do about it. "Because your mom doesn't want me to?"

"Because I don't want you to, okay?" She began to shake and tears dribbled from the corner of her eyes.

"Why, Mandy? Because you don't want medical equipment in your bedroom?"

"Yes!" The tears came faster and she angrily wiped them away. "I mean *no*, that's not the reason. It's just...don't buy it, damn it! Don't buy my house! Just *don't*." With a wail, she spun away from him.

He was stunned by her outburst. It was so unlike her to lose it. "Hey." He took hold of her quivering shoulders and turned her gently around. "Hey."

She clutched his shirt and buried her face against his chest.

"It's okay." He wrapped his arms around her. "It's okay, Buttercup." Then he held her while she soaked his shirt with her tears. He didn't have to guess what kind of tears they were. The reality of selling the house where she'd grown up hadn't hit her until he'd offered to buy it. She was grieving.

If he imagined his mom selling the ranch, he could somewhat grasp how much Mandy was hurting. For her it might be more complicated because of bad memories, but she still had fifteen years of her life tied up in that house. Detaching from it had to be tough.

He shared her pain as best he could and tried to comfort her. He rubbed her back and smoothed her hair. When he kissed the top of her head, he breathed in the coconut scent of her shampoo. She'd always liked coconut.

Leaning down, he pressed his lips to her temple. She snuffled and slid her arms around his neck. After that, he lost track of things. What he'd intended as comfort became something else as he kissed her wet cheek and she turned her head so he connected with her mouth.

Her lips were soft and moist, like rose petals after a rain. They parted easily, inviting him in. He tasted the salt of her tears and hesitated. She was distraught. He nibbled gently, waiting for her to change her mind.

Instead she whimpered and clutched the back of his head to pull him closer, deeper. God help him, he responded, thrusting his tongue into her mouth with a groan of surrender. Yes, oh, yes. *This.*

She arched against him, her body a warm, yielding promise. He lifted her up and she wrapped her legs around him. She belonged there, right there. He carried her to the bed, laying her down on the colorful squares of his handmade quilt.

She gazed up at him, her expression open and vulnerable.

Once again, he waited, giving her time, a moment to reconsider.

She swallowed. "Love me."

He'd never been so willing to answer a plea. He began to undress her and she watched him with luminous eyes. As the delicate scent of coconut teased him, he slowly revealed the swell of her breasts, the sweet curve of her hips, the tempting space between her silken thighs. He paused along the way to touch, to kiss, to taste. With every caress, her breath came faster.

When he removed the last of her clothes, she grasped his hand and her voice was barely a whisper. "Now you."

Standing, he pulled off his clothes and she followed every movement. The muted glow from the fire gave him just enough light to see the flush on her cheeks when he shoved down his briefs. Tossing them away, he took a package of condoms from the bedside table. He'd bought them more than a year ago. Never broke the seal.

He held her gaze as he ripped open a foil packet, rolled on a condom and climbed onto the bed. At each stage in this journey he'd expected her to balk, but when he moved between her thighs, she lifted her arms and welcomed him.

Sinking into her warmth was the most natural thing in the world, as if he'd been making love to her for years. Maybe they would have if things had turned out different. It didn't matter. He was grateful for this moment.

She didn't let him linger over it. Her body rose to meet his with an eagerness that sent heat shooting through his veins. The urgent press of her fingertips drove him on and he plunged into her over and over. Each time he made that connection, the jolt of sensation nearly took his head off.

Her wild cries and deep moans told him that he was getting it right, that he was loving her the way she needed to be loved. This was communication on a basic level in a language he'd never shared with her but which came to him instinctively.

He felt her tighten around his cock. She was ready to come. He could slow down and draw out the experience but he made a guess that she wouldn't want that. He gave it all he had, pounding into her until she reached a very noisy climax and he followed right after.

For a while their heavy breathing was the only sound in the room. He stayed balanced on his forearms as he slowly came to his senses. What now? With any other woman, he'd know what to say, what to do next.

But these were Mandy's thighs he was wedged tightly between. These were Mandy's breasts he brushed against whenever he moved even a little bit. He couldn't give her a lingering kiss and tell her she was amazing and the sex had been incredible. She was and it had been, but they still had issues to settle and they hadn't solved anything by getting naked.

Instead they'd complicated the hell out of the situation.

9

Now what? As the haze of lust gradually cleared, Mandy lay there, stunned by her own idiocy. How could she have allowed this to happen? After putting a stop to their ill-advised kiss yesterday she'd turned around and...and.... She couldn't even put words to what she'd done. As her breathing returned to normal, she kept her eyes closed because she couldn't bear to look up and see Zane staring down at her.

She was naked, and worse yet, *he* was naked. She'd never seen him without clothes but she certainly had, now. He was gorgeous, but still, he was *Zane.* She'd managed to set aside that pertinent fact while letting him undress her. She'd writhed beneath him without even a tiny bit of ladylike restraint. Because of her delusional thinking, she'd had the most satisfying orgasm of her life.

That part had been spectacular. But now that the glow had faded and her brain was functioning again, she had to deal with the fact that Zane had been intimately involved in that ecstatic moment. If he had any sensitivity at all he would leave the bed immediately without saying a single word so she could leap up, throw on her clothes and vamoose.

But no, he remained right where he'd been at the end of the action, although he wasn't talking, either. Maybe, like her, he was struggling with what was appropriate to say after having no-holds-barred sex with his former best friend. She had the answer for him. He should keep his mouth shut and allow them to regain a small portion of their dignity.

At least the lighting was dim and he wouldn't be able to see her naked self very well. That might not matter anymore, though. After asking him to love her—how embarrassing was that?—she'd let him remove every item of clothing from her body and kiss whatever areas he pleased. That had turned out to be quite a lot.

Dear God, this was beyond awkward. Why didn't he just move? Clearly he wasn't going to, so she'd have to be the one to get them out of this pickle. She cleared her throat. "Um, I should go."

"Sorry, what?" He sounded dazed and confused.

She found the courage to open her eyes. "I need to leave."

His face was in shadow. "You don't have to. You could—"

"I have to. I didn't leave a note for Mom." She'd intended to be out and back before her mother realized she'd been gone. But she'd been away much longer than she'd planned. And she'd done things she'd never, ever meant to do.

"Oh."

"So if you could just..."

"Right." It must have dawned on him that he was pinning her down. "I'll head into the bathroom."

He withdrew with care and climbed out of the bed. She grabbed the covers and pulled them up to her neck on the off chance he'd glance in her direction. He walked into the bathroom but didn't close the door, damn it.

She had to take advantage of this opportunity, regardless. Leaping out of bed, she located her panties but not her bra. She abandoned the search in favor of pulling on her jeans and her sweater. She crammed her feet into her boots and snatched up her jacket from the floor as he came out of the bathroom.

He hadn't taken any of his clothes with him so she was afraid to look. Instead she quickly put on her jacket. Her sweater sleeves bunched up because she shoved her arms in too fast but that was a small matter.

"You could send your mom a text if you think she might wake up and be worried."

"A text?" She searched the floor for her bra. "You mean tell her where I am?"

"What's wrong with that? She doesn't have to know that we—"

"I'm not texting her." She located her bra but had to take her phone out of her jacket pocket before she could stuff her bra inside. His comment made her decide to check the screen in case her mom had texted her, which would be bad. She hadn't.

"Hang on and I'll drive you."

Not happening. She couldn't imagine trying to ignore him while he put on his clothes. The room was getting smaller by the minute. "I'll be fine walking." She gave him a quick glance and was relieved that he'd had the decency to wrap a towel around his hips. Even so, there was a lot of male muscle on display.

She zipped her jacket and picked up her hat and scarf from the floor. Maybe if they hadn't had sex his nakedness wouldn't bother her so much, but what was done was done. She'd never be able to look him in the eye again. She started for the door.

"Mandy, let me drive you back. Or at least walk you over. Give me a minute to put on my clothes."

"No can do." A blast of cold air made her gasp when she opened the door.

"See? It's damned cold out there. Come back inside and wait for me."

"See ya." She made her getaway and prayed he wouldn't follow her. That was one advantage of leaving him while he wore only a towel. She jogged over to the path and race-walked once she was into the trees.

She didn't turn on her flashlight app until she tripped on a tree root and almost did a face plant. She'd known every inch of this path years ago but the forest had made a few changes. Anyway, she could slow down, now. Zane wouldn't follow her after she was already on her way. That would scare her to death and he'd know that.

He understood her too well, unfortunately. She'd contained her meltdown this morning only to have a spectacular one here. In the process, she'd revealed *way* too much, starting with her body.

But that wasn't all she'd let him see. Now they both knew she was still emotionally attached to the house and to him. His offer to buy her old home had touched off a landslide of memories and heartaches.

But as the walk helped clear away the mental and emotional debris, she thought about the comments he'd made before things got crazy. If she wanted her mom to move to New York, then someone else would live in the house. Like Zane said, the new owner could do whatever they wanted, including tearing the place down.

Maybe knowing what would happen to the house and who'd bought it would be slightly easier than imagining someone buying it for the land and taking a bulldozer to the house. She'd heard stories of families who'd sold a beloved home to a stranger and had returned later to find it gone.

Well, Zane McGavin was certainly no stranger. Now she knew him in the Biblical sense. But if she played her cards right, she'd never have to see him again. She had no plans to return to Eagles Nest.

But her mom probably would want to come back to visit friends. She'd drive out to the old house because that's what people did after they'd moved away. If Zane owned it, her mother could go inside and she'd know what to expect. She wouldn't get any nasty shocks.

An owl hooted in one of the tall pines along the path. Another one answered. Mandy hooted back. She'd perfected the technique as a kid but she was a little rusty. Even so, she got a response.

She and Zane used to love listening to the owls at night. Now he was dedicated to protecting them. When she looked at the house purchase from his point of view, her objections seemed irrational.

They probably were, and she'd shut up about it. But she still hated the idea that he'd occupy her former home, especially after what had just happened. How could she have allowed herself to have sex with him? What was wrong with her?

***

Zane had a restless night and woke early. He was more than ready to spend his day mucking out stalls and grooming horses. A trail ride was scheduled for the next day and the barn and the animals had to look shipshape. The weekend had crept up on him while he'd been obsessing over Mandy and the potential for buying Aunt Jo's house, but today he'd focus on the ranch's primary business.

Friday was traditionally the day to get organized for the trail rides, a significant moneymaker. Boarding provided a steady income and riding lessons brought in sporadic cash, but the trail rides, with anywhere from eight to ten people paying for a trip that would take most of the day, kept them in the black.

Over the years Wild Creek Ranch had built a reputation for excellent trail guides, dependable horses, and the best sack lunch anyone could ask for. His mom had the lunch routine down to a science and everyone who rode with them raved about the food.

Zane maintained the barn and the tack, and he took pride in clean stalls and well-oiled leather. He'd turned all the horses out first thing, even Winston. The Paint's foreleg looked strong and Zane was confident Winston could handle the trail the following day. With the barn empty, he could move faster as he cleaned out stalls and spread fresh straw in each one.

He'd left the doors open and he could hear his mom out in the arena schooling Licorice, a pretty little black mare with a bad attitude. A whinny of protest told him things weren't going well.

Indulgent parents had bought the mare for their twelve-year-old daughter because the girl had fallen in love with a Black Beauty lookalike. Retraining the contrary horse would take a lot of time and effort, but his mom had agreed to give it a try.

After about twenty minutes she came into the barn looking disgruntled.

Zane leaned on his rake. "Giving up?"

"No. Just taking a break and letting her have some time to think about her actions. She'll come around, but somebody sure let her get away with murder. Has she tried to bite you?"

"Not yet."

"Well, watch out for that, although she might not try it with you since you've never put a saddle on her. She's fine if she's treated like a pampered pet, but carrying a rider is not her thing. At least not yet."

"If anyone can change her mind, you can."

"Let's hope you're right. By the way, Jo called first thing this morning and asked if I could come over for lunch today. Normally I wouldn't leave you on a Friday, but I want to see Mandy again before she takes off. I may or may not tell her what I think about her plan, but this would give me a chance if I'm ever going to say something."

"Hey, no worries." He tried to sound casual, although any reference to Mandy was bound to put him on edge. "When is she leaving, by the way? I was never clear on that."

"Tuesday."

His gut tightened. "I guess that would be a week. It's gone fast."

"It has. She suggested Jo might want to put in her notice at the bank, but Jo isn't doing it yet. She wants to shepherd your loan through the system, which also serves as a stalling tactic."

"I appreciate it, no matter what her reasons are. The loan process should go fine, but knowing she's looking out for my interests is a comfort."

His mom smiled. "Of course she wants to help. It's in her best interests, too. She loves you and is thrilled that you're buying the house. On the phone this morning she raved about your plans."

"She did?" That was a relief. Mandy had implied Aunt Jo had reservations, but apparently not.

"She's very excited about the raptor headquarters. I'll admit at first I was reluctant for you to take on such a big obligation but I'm on board with it, now."

"Good to hear." So only one person opposed his plan and she'd be gone by Tuesday. He should be happy about that.

His mom heaved a sigh and glanced toward the arena. "Okay, I can't justify putting this off any longer. I need to get back to Miss Bitchy."

He laughed. "That fits her better than Licorice."

"You're telling me. There's nothing sweet about that mare, but I'm being paid well to teach her manners and I will by God do it." She started out of the barn but turned back. "I'm sure Jo will have dessert. I'll bring you some."

"Great idea."

"I'm full of them." She gave him a wave and left the barn.

Zane went back to raking, but the discussion had brought up exactly the person and situation he'd been trying to forget. He'd been willing to leave Mandy alone, but she'd come marching over to see him and now...he'd remember last night for the rest of his life, damn it. Judging from the way she'd hightailed it out of his cabin, she never wanted a repeat, either.

But she'd started it. If she hadn't come knocking on his door they wouldn't have had sex and he wouldn't be haunted by that episode. The imprint of her body and the scent of her skin had stayed with him even after he'd slept, showered, and put on different clothes. Unless he wanted to toss and turn tonight, he'd have to change the sheets before he went to bed.

She'd messed with him. Yes, he could have resisted the impulse to hold her while she cried, but he hadn't been raised that way. Then one thing had led to another and while he could have backed away at any point, she'd encouraged him to keep going. Now he couldn't stop thinking about it.

He hoped she was as tortured by that roll in the hay as he was. If she was blithely going about her day without giving him another thought, that would suck. If she could fly back to the big city on Tuesday without a single regret, that would—

A sharp cry from the arena made him toss away the rake and start down the barn aisle.

"Zane!"

He took off running. His mom wasn't the type to panic, so something awful had happened out there. He bolted through the double doors and saw her on the ground. Licorice stood on the other side of the arena looking innocent. Ha. That damned horse had thrown her, sure as the world. And she wasn't getting up.

He hurried through the gate and latched it behind him. They didn't need a loose animal adding to the problem. "What happened?"

His mom's face was white and her jaw was clenched. "She threw me. Landed on my leg."

He crouched beside her. "How bad?"

"I think... *damn.*" She gasped in pain. "Zane, when I fell, something snapped. I think my leg's broken."

10

Mandy and her mom had decided to bake a chocolate layer cake to serve after lunch. Or rather, her mom had decided and Mandy had gone along with it.

Normally she'd look forward to having lunch with Aunt Kendra, but not today. She got out two cake pans and wax paper for lining them while her mother mixed the batter in a big yellow bowl with scratches on the sides from years of constant use.

The bowl was something Mandy figured should make the move to New York. As kids, she and Zane had been allowed to clean it with spoons after the cake batter or cookie dough was gone. Her mom used to hand them each a beater to lick, too. That childhood memory made last night seem even more unreal.

But it hadn't been a dream, as she'd first hoped when she'd opened her eyes early this morning. She'd showered to wash away his scent, but her body was still sensitized. Every time she thought about him, which happened with embarrassing regularity, her nipples tightened and her lady parts tingled.

"Mandy, are you all right?"

Startled, she glanced at her mother and then at the wax paper in her hand. She hadn't finished her job and her mom was ready to pour the batter. "Sorry. I got distracted." She quickly lined both pans. "There you go."

Her mom efficiently divided the batter between the pans. "I know you're not happy about Zane's idea, but I'm hoping it'll grow on you." She slid the pans into the hot oven. "To be honest, I was a little surprised at how upset you were." She rinsed the bowl and put it in the dishwasher.

"I'm not as dead-set against it as I was yesterday."

Turning, her mom gazed at her. "Did you and Zane work it out?"

Her cheeks grew hot. "Um, I'm not sure what you mean."

"I heard you leave last night and there's only one place I could think of you'd go."

The years fell away and she was sixteen again. "I hope I didn't worry you."

"I wasn't worried. You're a big girl and this is a small town. I just hope you and Zane have come to an understanding."

How in the world was she supposed to respond to *that*? "We...um..."

"Never mind, sweetie. I don't have to know the details. But Kendra and I hate it when you two aren't getting along. He *is* going to buy this house and it'll be better all the way around if you're okay with that."

She nodded. "I will be. I just—" She paused when her mom's phone rang. Saved by the bell.

"Excuse me a minute." Her mom reached for the phone lying on the counter and glanced at the screen. "It's Zane." She answered with a smile that quickly turned to a gasp of dismay. "Oh, no. How awful! We'll be right there. Yes. 'Bye." She disconnected.

"What happened?"

"A horse threw Kendra and she's broken her leg. Zane took her to the emergency room." She switched off the oven but didn't stop long enough to take out the cake pans. "Let's go. I'll drive."

Mandy raced into her room, picked up the jacket she'd worn the night before and her purse before following her mother out the front door. "Did he say how bad it is?"

"Lower leg is all I know."

"That's probably better than upper leg, right?"

"Neither is any damn good." Her mom hopped in the SUV and Mandy hurried to get in on the other side. She'd barely fastened her seatbelt before her mom had backed around and started down the rutted road going fast.

"I hate this for her, Mandy. The physical pain is bad enough, but she can't lead trail rides or work in the barn with a broken leg."

Mandy couldn't remember ever being in the car with her mom when she drove like this. She swerved around most of the ruts but hit a few.

If Mandy hadn't been buckled in she would have banged her head on the roof.

Once they made it to the paved road, her mom picked up her phone and called someone. "Hey. Kendra was thrown and broke her leg. I'm headed to the emergency room." She paused. "No, we probably shouldn't all show up, but I'm thinking we need to schedule a gathering at her house tonight. She's gonna be feeling like hell and we need to help her through the first night. Yep. Five-thirty's good. Bring food. And wine, although she can't have any, poor thing. See you then." She hung up the phone.

Mandy stared at her mother in astonishment. "Who was that?"

"Deirdre."

"Do I know her?"

"I'm sure you've met her, but it's been awhile. She's one of Kendra's friends from high school."

"I'm not pulling up a mental image." But judging from that quick conversation, her mother was very close to this Deidre person.

"She's short, on the plump side, has brown hair but lately she's been dying it red. Got divorced about five years ago. Loves to laugh. She used to come out to Kendra's with her kids when you were there playing with the McGavin boys, but her children are younger than you. I think the oldest is twenty-two."

Mandy had no memory of this person but she might if she saw her face or heard her voice. "What's this about a party at Aunt Kendra's tonight?"

"It's what we usually do when one of us has a crisis."

"What do you mean by *we*?"

Her mom kept glancing in her rearview mirror, probably because she was doing at least fifteen miles over the speed limit. "I'm trying to remember if I ever mentioned the Whine and Cheese Club."

"Don't think so. Want me to help look for cops?"

"Please. I could talk my way out of a ticket but I don't want to take the time. Anyway, the Whine and Cheese Club isn't exactly a club. It's just me, Kendra, Deidre, Christine and Judy. Everybody graduated the same year from ENHS except me. Those four are best friends and Kendra generously invited me to be part of the group."

"Boy, I don't remember that at all."

"I didn't hang out with them much when I was married to your father. He didn't approve. But when he and I separated they became my lifeline. They cheered me on through the divorce."

"That's...that's good. I'm glad." She certainly hadn't been much help, especially in the beginning. "I'm just surprised I never heard about them."

"Whenever you've come home it's always been for such a short time and I didn't want to dilute it by bringing them into the picture. They understood."

Mandy could think of another reason her mom hadn't included her in a gathering with these women. The group included Aunt Kendra and her mom had known Mandy had been avoiding the McGavins. "They sound nice."

"They are nice."

"But are you sure about this party thing?" She continued to digest the revelation that her mother was surrounded by a supportive group of women. She'd thought Aunt Kendra was her only close friend. "I can't believe Aunt Kendra will feel like partying."

"Think about it. This will be her first night to figure everything out, like how to manage crutches if she has them, how to make it to the bathroom, how to take a bath or shower. I'm not sure how any of that works but it's got to be tricky. Zane's great, but she probably won't want him to help her take a bath."

"I guess you're right."

"With us she doesn't have to watch her language. She can swear a blue streak if she wants. We'll get her to see the funny side of it. Otherwise she's liable to become depressed when she thinks of all she can't do. We won't let her dwell on anything, at least not tonight."

"Am I invited?"

"Of course you are! You can meet everyone. Well, we're here!" She parked in the lot nearest the emergency entrance. "I think I set a new record."

"I don't doubt it. I've never seen you drive like that."

"I can when it's important. Oh, and FYI, your bra's dangling out of your jacket pocket."

"Shit!" Face hotter than a stove burner, she shoved it inside while her mother laughed.

"Great comic relief, sweetie. Thanks." Her mom opened her door. "Let's go."

Taking a deep breath, she exited her mom's SUV. She saw Zane's truck three spaces over and felt a hum low in her belly. "Mom, I'd appreciate it if you wouldn't tell Aunt Kendra that Zane and I..."

"I won't." As they started toward the hospital, she wrapped an arm around Mandy's shoulders. "But this explains why you've been acting a little weird."

"That's because it *is* weird. He used to be my best friend."

"That doesn't have to change." She gave Mandy's shoulder a squeeze. "But Kendra's our priority right now."

"Absolutely." She held the door for her mother and walked in behind her. The Eagles Nest Hospital didn't look much different from when she'd been rushed here when she was eight with a gash in her arm. She'd fallen on the rocks while playing along Wild Creek with the boys. The antiseptic smell, the polished floors and the sea-green walls brought back that memory. She still had a faint scar.

Her mom checked her phone. "Zane just texted. He'll meet us in the waiting room. They only let one person at a time back there with Kendra."

"Makes sense." She followed her mom into the small lounge furnished with utilitarian sofas and chairs upholstered in imitation leather that could be sanitized easily. A family with a couple of small children had camped out in one corner surrounded by the remains of a fast food lunch. The parents were on their phones and the kids were concentrating on their coloring books.

Mandy's mother glanced at them and smiled. "Takes me back."

"To what?"

"When you cut your arm, your father was away on a business trip. Kendra packed up her boys and drove us over here. She always had a tote bag loaded with quiet time activities. She kept those boys amused until we were ready to go."

"I was probably crying too hard to remember any of that."

"Yep, you were pretty upset. So was Zane. He—ah, here he is."

Mandy turned and met his somber gaze as he walked toward them. Her first instinct was to give him a hug, but she hesitated. Everything was different, now. Zane and her mom embraced with the familiarity of old friends while Mandy stood by and wondered how in hell to navigate this situation.

"Kendra's a tough cookie," her mother said. "This'll be just a blip on the radar."

"That's exactly what she told me." Zane rubbed the back of his neck. "It's a clean break of both the tibia and fibula. I just learned those words, by the way."

Her heart went out to him. He looked so worried, poor guy. She might not feel comfortable hugging him, but she could offer help. "Is there anything we can do? I know you must have left in a hurry. Is there something that needs to be handled at the ranch?"

He glanced at her as if trying to process the question. "You know, there is, and I wish I'd thought of it before you made the trip in."

"Never mind that. I can go back and take care of whatever it is."

"I need the trail ride list so I can start calling folks. It should be lying on the desk."

"I'll get it." Mandy took the car keys her mother held out.

"There's one other problem." Zane scrubbed a hand over his face. "I left the mare in the arena. You'll probably notice that when you drive in."

"She's still tacked up?"

"I hope so. No telling what she might have done after we left." He pulled out his phone. "But you don't need to deal with her. I'll call—"

"Don't be silly. I'll take care of her while I'm out there."

"I don't know. That mare's a handful. Mom said she bites."

"No worries. Eeyore used to bite."

"He did?" Zane frowned. "I don't remember that."

"And I never knew it." Her mom gave her a look.

"I was afraid you'd make me get rid of him. He wasn't always as sweet as he is now. I had to work with him." She turned toward Zane. "I can handle the mare. What's her name?"

"Licorice."

"Cute."

"Yeah, well, she's not. I don't want anything happening to you." His gaze was filled with concern and something else, a flicker of awareness that was growing stronger by the second.

Her breath caught. When they were kids she'd been able to read him pretty well. Today he was even more transparent. She'd bet he was thinking about what had happened between them, and now she was, too. "I'll be careful."

"Please do." He reached over and touched her arm. "Text me after you get her in the stall."

"I will." Pulse racing, she made her getaway. It seemed she didn't have to worry about embarrassment where Zane was concerned. She hadn't blushed when she'd seen that telltale warmth in his eyes. No sir. She'd wanted to push him into the nearest broom closet and kiss him senseless.

The drive to the ranch gave her time to cool off. She didn't drive back at her mom's breakneck speed, but she made good time. She found Licorice standing by the gate looking forlorn, reins dangling to the ground. Normally, Mandy would have been sympathetic, but this was the animal that had sent Aunt Kendra to the emergency room.

Opening the gate, she got a tight grip on the bridle so the mare couldn't bite her. "You're in a heap of trouble, Licorice." She gathered up the reins and looped them around the saddle horn. "You'd better behave yourself if you know what's good for you." She had nothing to back up that threat, but a firm tone was usually helpful.

She led the horse straight to the barn, put her in the nearest empty stall and closed her in. "I need to fetch a halter. No funny business, okay?"

Clearly Licorice was affected by the circumstances, because for a horse that was supposed to be feisty she acted subdued. When Mandy came back, the mare was in the same spot. She continued her docile behavior while Mandy unsaddled her and replaced the bridle with a halter.

She glanced at the mare's dusty coat. "You could use a good brushing, but I don't have time for that. I'm heading back to the hospital to see the woman who has a broken leg because of you."

Licorice gazed at her. Mandy imagined she saw regret in those brown eyes. Then the mare tried to nip her arm and she ducked out of the stall and latched the door. "If I were sticking around, I'd take you on as a personal challenge. I'm kind of sorry I won't be able to."

After sending Zane a quick text that Licorice was safely in a stall, she left the barn and walked up to the house. The list was right where Zane had said it would be because the office was tidy. That would help in the coming weeks, but running this operation without Aunt Kendra's full participation would be a challenge.

The accident could have a ripple effect—altering Zane's plans to buy the house and her mom's timetable for moving out of it. Would her mom want to stay until Aunt Kendra was back on her feet? She might.

Mandy would like to have her mother living in New York within a month or so. She'd checked out summer festivals and new plays that were opening. But she also loved Aunt Kendra. Her mom would be a comfort during the recovery period.

A delay in the plan seemed likely, not to mention that her mom hadn't officially agreed to the move. Once she did, that would simplify things.

Before returning to the hospital she made a quick detour home so she could toss the incriminating bra in the laundry hamper. No doubt her mom had suspected what had gone on last night before she'd had it confirmed by the dangling bra.

Mandy sighed. Moving her mother should have been a slam dunk but it wasn't turning out that way. The harder she tried, the more things got effed up.

11

Zane relaxed when Mandy came into the waiting room. Her text had helped him figure her ETA so he'd walked out to meet her. She was good with horses, but that mare was trouble.

Thankfully Mandy was fine. More than fine. She was...beautiful. She must have rushed out of the house this morning, and yet she was gorgeous, all the same. She'd been gorgeous yesterday when she'd appeared in a hot pink t-shirt and tight jeans. He'd even liked the messy hairstyle.

When he'd discovered her stranded on the road, she'd been decked out like the city girl she'd become, but since then she'd reverted to the Mandy he knew best, the one he...no, better not go there.

She hurried toward him. "How's she doing?"

"They're putting the cast on. Your mom is with her and talking up a storm. We've been trading off since you left, trying to take her attention away from that damned cast. It'll be like a ball and chain. Worse than one, actually."

"But that's how she'll heal."

"You're right." He took off his hat and ran his hands through his hair. "I just wish...well, it doesn't matter what I wish, does it?" He put his hat back on. "Listen, I can't thank you enough for driving out there and taking care of Licorice. Did she give you any trouble?"

"Not really. Except when I started thinking she was harmless and let down my guard a little she tried to nip me. I have good reflexes, though. She didn't succeed."

He clenched his fists. "I think Licorice needs to be boarded with someone else. I don't want her around."

"But your stable is the best in the area. If any horse needs extra TLC, Licorice does."

"I'm not in the mood to give that mare anything extra." Arguing about the horse kept him from doing something stupid, like hauling her into his arms. Not a good idea. He wasn't entirely in control where Mandy was concerned. "Licorice would be better off with someone who doesn't look at her and remember his mom lying on the ground with a broken leg."

"It's not her fault, Zane." Her tone was gentle rather than challenging. She didn't sound like she was trying to start a fight. More like she was advocating for the horse.

"Maybe not, but her best hope for a change of attitude is currently having a cast put on her leg. Even if I wanted to tackle the job, Licorice doesn't like men. She barely tolerates women but men really get her dander up."

"I wish I could do it."

"I wish you could, too." Whoops. He'd said that with way too much enthusiasm. "I mean, I wish you could magically keep your job in New York and whisk yourself out here several times a week to train Licorice." *And make love to me.*

"Wouldn't that be nice? Being around horses is one of the things I've missed."

He'd like to know if being around him was another thing she'd missed, but he wouldn't ask. Whichever way she answered would create problems. "Did you find the list?"

"Yep." She pulled the folded sheet out of her purse. "I can help you make the calls if you want. My phone's charged."

"I may take you up on that. I had a long talk with Cody that sucked a lot of battery life and naturally I didn't bring my charger. It's a wonder I remembered my phone."

"Is he driving down?"

"He doesn't know yet. He committed to helping with an event at the dude ranch and he's not sure if he can get out of it. I told him not to worry if he can't. She'll be in this condition for a while so anytime he can visit will be welcome."

"So Cody's a maybe and Ryker is out of the country until August. When are Trevor and Bryce coming back from Texas?"

"Last I heard it was indefinite. The guy who hired them has a big ranch and those two are good hands. They're making great money, too, so I'm holding off calling them about Mom. They might quit and drive back. She wouldn't want that."

"I think you're right to wait."

"I'll tell them you said so when they chew my ass about it later." He gazed at her. She had such expressive eyes. They were filled with sympathy and he soaked it up, but he had to be careful not to appear needy. He was still smarting from the way she'd cut out on him last night.

"So it's just you holding down the fort."

"Pretty much."

"You and the Whine and Cheese ladies."

He smiled. "Yeah, they'll be a big help with Mom, but can you picture any of those women mucking out a stall?"

"I don't know. I've never met them."

"You haven't? How come?"

"Mom said it was because my visits have been so short." She paused. "I think it was so I wouldn't have an awkward meeting with your mom."

"Oh." Damn, she looked sad.

"My own fault."

"I'll bet you'll meet them this time."

"Yep. Tonight, in fact. They're coming over to the ranch house around five-thirty to help Aunt Kendra adjust to this new development. I got the impression they'll pull an all-nighter."

"I should have figured on that."

She peered up at him. "You're okay with it?"

"Sure. I was wondering if I'd need to bunk in the house tonight but this is better. They'll make her laugh and that's way more important than anything else. They'll be a big help while we work through this thing."

"Mom said they were a big help to her when she went through the divorce."

"I think they were." He would tread carefully. That period was filled with land mines.

"I had this idea that except for Aunt Kendra, Mom was sort of isolated after the divorce."

"Not really." He considered stating the obvious, that her mom had a full life in Eagles Nest with friends she'd known for years, but he didn't have the heart to push her buttons right now.

She dragged in a breath. "Okay, what's the plan? Do you want my phone? Should I go relieve Mom?"

"Yes, and yes. Let's head back there so I can show you where she is."

"Maybe I should tell her some jokes."

"That depends." He ushered her through the double doors and into the corridor. "You used to be famous for forgetting the punch line."

"Not the ones for my specialty jokes."

Oh, yeah. He'd forgotten about those. "Nix on the knock-knock jokes, Buttercup."

"I'll bet she'd laugh."

He took her arm and pulled her to a stop. "If you're planning to torture that poor woman when she can't escape, then I'm not taking you back there."

"Knock-knock."

"I'm not playing. This isn't the time for—"

"Come on. You know you want to. Knock-knock."

He rolled his eyes. "Who's there?"

"Hoo."

"Who who?" It was just dumb enough to break through his crappy mood and make him smile. "I can't believe I fell for that."

"See? It's so silly it works. Take me to Aunt Kendra. She needs to hear my jokes."

"Maybe so." He hadn't seen the goofy side of Mandy in a long time. He'd wondered if he ever would again. "If she tells you to stop, promise me you will."

"Never fear. I love your mom." She walked with him down the corridor. "That who-who joke reminds me that on my way home last night the owls were hooting."

Her casual reference to last night brought him up short and he sucked in a breath.

She put her hand on his arm. "I'm sorry."

"About what?" He wondered if she was going to apologize for coming to his cabin.

"I shouldn't have mentioned the owls."

She looked so remorseful that he almost reached for her. Then he remembered they were standing in a hospital corridor with people passing by. "Why not? Hearing the owls is very cool."

"Yes, but it's not helpful to bring up a topic related to last night when you're probably trying to forget it ever happened." She glanced away. "You might even wish it never had."

"This morning I wished exactly that."

"Oh, Zane." She gazed up at him, her voice filled with regret. "It was all my fault."

"Not *all* your fault." He hesitated. "The thing is, I don't wish that anymore. But you probably do."

"I thought I did. Now, though...well, it happened and we can't do anything about it, so what's the point in wishing it away?"

"No point." He wanted to hold her more than he wanted to breathe.

"But it's changed everything between us."

"It changed a long time ago, Buttercup."

"I know and I hate that. I've missed you."

His heart lurched. "I've missed you, too. Maybe...maybe we could start changing it back."

"How?"

He took a deep breath. "For one thing, we used to be able to say anything to each other, but now I censor myself."

"Me, too."

"We should stop doing that."

"We should." She paused. "All right, here goes. Does Aunt Kendra's accident mean you won't buy our house?"

"I don't know yet. I hope not. Would you be happy if I didn't?"

"I don't know. Maybe."

He nodded. "Fair enough. Anything else you want to say before we head back to see Mom?"

"You look really hot today."

He choked on a laugh and had to clear his throat before he could speak. "So do you."

* * *

Mandy had no time to think about Zane after she handed him her phone and took her mom's place in the curtained cubicle. Aunt Kendra didn't look as perky as she had the last time Mandy had seen her, but she showed remarkable courage under fire.

She laughed at Mandy's knock-knock jokes and she wasn't faking it, either. Maybe the jokes were why she seemed so cheerful about the damage to her favorite work jeans, which had been sliced along the seam when she'd been brought in. The nurse pinned the jeans back in place to keep her patient from mooning everybody when she practiced walking with her crutches in the hallway.

Aunt Kendra declared the jeans were good as new. But Mandy knew clothing and those jeans would never fit the same. If she could take them back to New York with her, she might be able to recreate them. She'd give it a shot because perfect-fitting jeans didn't come along every day.

The crutches turned into quite a challenge. The doctor offered a wheelchair but Aunt Kendra firmly rejected that option. Instead she practiced with the crutches, going up and down the corridor with Mandy by her side ready to catch her if she started to fall.

The sun was low in the sky when it was finally time for the trip home. Everyone concluded the SUV was a better bet than Zane's truck. Getting the injured passenger inside and positioned on the back seat with her leg propped up was a trick, but Zane's muscles came in handy and they managed it.

After his mom was as comfortable as possible, he leaned in and gave her a kiss on the cheek. "See you at home."

"Thanks, Zaneman."

He chuckled and shook his head before loping over to his truck.

Zaneman? Mandy never remembered hearing that before, but then she hadn't interacted with either of them for ten years. She climbed into the passenger seat and turned so that she could keep an eye on Aunt Kendra during the ride back. She gave her an encouraging smile. "How're you doing?"

"Perfectamundo, Mandy-Wandy."

"Uh, that's good, I guess." She glanced over at her mother.

Her mom grinned as she turned the key. "They increased the dosage on her pain meds so she could tolerate the trip home. She's high as a kite."

"Yes, yes I am!" Their backseat passenger put both hands in the air. "Wheeee."

Okay, so drugs were a big part of her cheerful attitude. She was a very brave woman. Stoned, but brave.

"Hey, Mandy-Wandy."

Mandy ignored her mother's snort and turned toward the back seat. "What?"

"Don't take Jo to New York, okay?"

"I won't take her now, that's for sure." That clinched it. The move would be delayed.

"Thanks, Mandy-Wandy. Hey, knock, knock."

"Who's there?"

"Boo."

"Boo who?"

"Gotcha! Hey, Josie-Wosie, it's karaoke time!" Aunt Kendra launched into a rendition of "Big Girls Don't Cry."

To Mandy's astonishment, her mom jumped in with a pretty darned good falsetto. The two women belted out the song as if they'd been singing together for years. Maybe they had been, although Mandy couldn't remember ever hearing them do it. Must have started after she'd left town.

Then they switched to "Girls Just Want to Have Fun." She knew the words to that one because she'd grown up listening to her mom's eighties music. She joined in and her mother flashed her a grin of delight. Mandy had never seen her looking like...like a *teenager*. They made it through "Livin' on a Prayer" and "I Wanna Dance with Somebody" before they pulled up in front of the ranch house.

Zane had beat them there and he opened the back door of the SUV. "How's it going, ladies?"

"I wanna dance with somebody!"

He braced his hands on the roof of the SUV and peered in at his mother. "I promise you'll be dancing before you know it, Mom."

"Oh, goodie." She stared at her cast. "Maybe not today, though."

"Maybe not. But I'd consider it an honor if you'd let me carry you into the house."

"An honor?" She placed a hand dramatically on her chest. "Then how can I possibly refuse?"

"That's the idea."

Mandy and her mom stood by to help, but Zane had the process under control. With gentleness and dexterity, he eased Aunt Kendra out of the backseat and carried her inside. Clearly the pain medication was still working because she gave him an animated description of how they'd sliced up her jeans and pinned them back together so they'd be like new.

Mandy hauled in the crutches and her mom carried the bag of medical supplies and instructions provided by the hospital. Zane settled his mother on the couch and positioned a small table next to her.

"See this, Mandy-Wandy?" Aunt Kendra gestured to the table and the afghan Zane had spread over her. "That's how I used to set things up for my boys when they were sick. Now Zaneman's doing the same thing for me. Isn't that sweet?"

"It sure is." She glanced at Zane as he left to get a pitcher of water and a glass. She hoped he was doing okay. The reality of the situation must be hitting him about now.

He came back with the water pitcher and glass. "I know she needs this." He looked at Mandy and her mother. "Do you remember what else is on the list?"

"No," her mom said. "But we can take it from here. Deidre should arrive any minute. Christine and Judy are on the way."

Mandy turned toward the grandfather clock in the corner and was shocked to discover it was nearly five-thirty. No wonder her stomach was rumbling. She hadn't eaten since breakfast.

Aunt Kendra perked up. "Is it Whine and Cheese night?"

"Yep!" Mandy's mom smiled at her. "Isn't that a coincidence?"

"Boy howdy, it sure is. Does everyone know I broke my leg?"

"I believe they do."

"We certainly do." A short, plump woman with red hair appeared in the doorway. "But listen here, girlfriend." She crossed the room and leaned over Aunt Kendra. "When you feel like having a Whine and Cheese party, just say so. We don't need you to go breaking your leg so we have an excuse."

"Worked like a fucking charm, didn't it?" Then she clapped her hand over her mouth and gave Zane a horrified glance.

He laughed until he was gasping for breath. "Okay, okay. I see it's time for me to leave you ladies to it. Anyway, I need to bring the horses in and feed them."

"I'll help you." The words were out of Mandy's mouth before she gave herself time to think.

"Thanks, but I've got it."

"No, seriously." She started toward him. "It'll go faster with two of us."

He gazed at her. "Then sure. That would be great."

"Hold on." Deidre hurried toward them. "Before you two leave, I want to introduce myself to the fabled daughter. I'm Deidre. Pleased to meet you." She grasped Mandy's hand in both of hers.

"Same here." Mandy met the woman's friendly gaze. Deidre might know her mother better than she did. That was disconcerting. "I'll be back after I help Zane."

"Great." Deidre gave her hand a squeeze. "See you soon."

Zane held the door for her as they walked out into the cool night air. "You don't have to do this."

"I know. I want to. I can check on Licorice."

He fell into step beside her. "Okay, but then you can go back to the party."

"What about you? What will you do tonight?"

He shrugged. "Head back to the cabin. Rustle up some food. I'm pretty hungry."

"Yeah, me, too."

"Then let's get 'er done."

Mandy had a blast helping Zane with the horses. She'd forgotten how chatty he was with the animals, especially a Paint named Winston. Zane handed her some gloves and she worked in tandem with him delivering hay flakes. She took the side of the barn Licorice was on so Zane wouldn't have to deal with her.

"This is great exercise," she called out to him about halfway through the process.

"Now there's a concept. Instead of hiring an extra hand, I'll bill the chores as a workout for fitness buffs and charge them. What d'ya think, Winston?"

The Paint answered with a loud snort and Mandy laughed. "Nice try, McGavin. Do you have any prospects for the job?"

"There's a high school kid we've hired the past couple of summers during our busy time, so if I can manage the barn until school's out, he's the logical choice."

"What about the trail rides until then?" He'd lose a ton of business and income between now and summer if he had to suspend the trail rides.

"That's trickier. I can't ask the high school kid because he uses his weekends to study and I can't just hire somebody off the street. I need to have complete confidence in whoever's riding with me. I'll think about it."

"I'm sure you'll work it out."

"I will. Takes time."

Time away from his raptor project. Poor guy had a lot to deal with right now. Helping him tonight wasn't much, but she was glad she could do it.

When they finished, he doused the overhead lights and closed the barn doors. Then he stood with her under a sky spangled with stars. Light streamed from the windows of the house and the faint sound of eighties music drifted toward them. "I'll walk you back." He started up the hill.

"Hang on a minute."

He paused and turned to her. "What?"

"I just realized I don't want to spend the night with the Whine and Cheese ladies."

"Why not? They're terrific."

"I'm sure they are, but—"

"They're expecting you."

"I know, but it's not like they need me." But Zane might. "Besides, I'll be the outsider. It'll feel sort of awkward."

"No, it won't. You're Aunt Jo's daughter. They'll welcome you with open arms."

"Of course they will, but they have a history that I don't share. Inside jokes I won't get. I can't possibly catch up in one night."

"So what's the alternative? Go back to your mom's house by yourself? They're not going to let you do that."

"No." The picture snapped into focus. "My mom cooked a big pot of veggie soup for lunch." She gazed up at him. "How does that sound for dinner?"

"Like heaven on earth. When you go in, ask your mom if I can drive over and steal some."

"I have a better idea. I'll tell her I invited you to have dinner at our house."

He stared at her for a long time. Then he cleared his throat. "Dinner at your house. You and me. Alone."

"Uh-huh."

"Mandy, if you're thinking we'll have dinner and then play Monopoly..."

She looked him straight in the eye. "No, I was thinking we'd have dinner and then have sex."

12

Zane gulped. "All righty, then."

"I'll be back in a flash." She smiled. "Wait here."

"I need to take care of the birds." *And grab condoms.*

"Want me to meet you up there?"

"No. I'll be quick. But if you beat me back, just wait in the truck. It's getting cold." He was vaguely aware of that although he felt hotter than a Halloween bonfire.

He accomplished his chores in record time but even so she was sitting in the passenger side of his truck when he made it down the hill. He'd been short on air ever since she'd dropped this bombshell of an idea. He climbed behind the wheel and took a deep breath. "What'd your mom say?"

"She told us to have fun." She held up a bottle of wine.

"Wow. Do you think she knows what—"

"She does, but the rest don't."

"You told her?"

"Didn't have to. I wore the same jacket to the emergency room and she saw my bra sticking out of the pocket."

"When was this? I didn't see anything sticking out."

"She told me before we got out of the car, so I shoved it in deeper."

"But when you walked into the hospital, it was in your pocket?"

"I wasn't going to take it out and leave it in my mom's SUV."

"It's a damn good thing I didn't know. I was having enough trouble blocking out the image of you lying naked on my bed." He shoved the key in the ignition and started the truck.

"Guys are so visual."

"And you're not?"

"Well, um, sometimes, maybe."

"You checked me out. I saw you do it." He backed around and started down the ranch road.

"I did. But then, afterward, I freaked out."

"I noticed. You pulled the covers up the minute I got out of bed. That's why I came out of the bathroom wearing a towel."

"For which I was grateful."

"You don't like seeing a guy's package?"

"Sure I do, but it seems wrong to look at yours!"

"Why?"

"Because...because you're *Zane,* the boy I used to build forts with and beat at Monopoly. We were all about board games and snowball fights. It was never about *sex.*"

Talk about confusing. "Are you sure you want me to come over tonight?"

"Yes!"

"Why?"

"For one thing, it doesn't seem fair that you should be all by yourself after such a traumatic day, and for another thing, I can't stop thinking about last night."

"That makes two of us. But maybe you should lay out the rules before we get there. Would you rather do it in the dark?"

Silence.

"Buttercup? Would you be less embarrassed if we doused the lights?"

"The thing is, although I did look, it was kind of dim lighting."

He laughed. Couldn't help it. "So, lights turned on?" Speaking of turned on...this discussion was heating up fast. Good thing her house wasn't far away.

"Yes. But is it going to be totally weird if we do it in my bedroom?"

"Not for me." His jeans were getting damned tight in the crotch. He wondered how she'd feel about doing it in the truck in about two minutes.

"I know. We'll haul my mattress into the living room. That'll be better."

"Okay." He'd haul it up to the roof if that would make her happy. "Listen, I know I said I was hungry, but..."

"You want to eat afterward?"

"Yes, ma'am."

"I think that can be arranged."

He let out a breath. "Good."

"But we're moving the mattress."

"Got it." But once they were inside the house, he discovered that was easier said than done. He stood in her bedroom staring at a queen-sized innerspring. Now he understood why earlier she'd wanted to clear such a large area in front of the fireplace. "Didn't you used to have a twin?" He reached up to tug on the brim of his hat and remembered he'd left it on the coat tree by the front door.

"I used to have a trundle bed but Mom upgraded me after my dad moved out."

"Guess I didn't know that."

"You weren't coming over by then."

"I suppose not." He glanced at her. She was so much more beautiful than she had been in high school. Her features had lost their rounded teenage look to become stronger and more defined. The girl he'd known had turned into a woman, one he wanted more than he would have imagined possible.

This time their lovemaking would be slow and easy. Instead of driving for the goal, he'd cherish every moment she'd give him. He told himself there was no rush to get started, but they were standing side-by-side in a room with a very inviting bed. "You're sure you want it out of here?"

"Yes. This room is stuffed with memories. Let me pull off the bedding."

While she accomplished that, he focused on a picture hanging on the wall so he wouldn't think about what they would be doing on that mattress. He recognized the view. They'd seen it yesterday from the lookout. "You took that, right?"

She stopped to look at it. "Sophomore year when I was in photography club. I'm so used to it I forgot it was there. Want it?"

"You don't?"

She studied it a moment. "No. If you like it, it's yours."

That bothered him. The lookout was their special place and one she'd appreciated enough to print and frame a picture she'd taken on one of their rides up there. The lookout was where they'd first kissed, although that hadn't ended well. But if they'd never kissed, they might not be moving a mattress tonight. "I'll take the picture."

She met his gaze. "You sound upset."

"I guess I'm more sentimental than you."

"You can afford to be."

That knocked him back. He remembered the ugly story of her dad's rejection, which helped explain why she wouldn't be keeping a bunch of souvenirs. If she succeeded in moving Aunt Jo to New York and severing her last tie, she'd never have to set foot in Eagles Nest again. He sighed. "You're right. Sorry."

"It's okay." She gathered up the sheets and comforter. "Ready."

"Stand back." He wrestled the mattress off the bed and onto its side. "Go ahead of me and guide it so we don't scrape paint off the walls."

"You're the one planning to buy the place. Do you care?"

"When you put it that way, no. Coming through." He shoved the mattress down the hall and into the living room. Once there he lowered it to the floor in front of the fireplace and helped her spread the sheets and comforter on top.

A manufactured log wrapped in paper sat on the grate. He briefly considered lighting it for atmosphere. Then he looked over at Mandy and scuttled the idea. They didn't need atmosphere. They could create their own.

She stood at the opposite end of the mattress, her body language telegraphing pride and a whisper of defiance. But her expression was filled with yearning. She was a bundle of contradictions that somehow reminded him of the golden eagle he'd rescued from the baling twine. He couldn't repair all the damage life had caused her, but maybe he could ease her pain.

He unsnapped the cuffs of his western shirt and watched her shrug out of her blouse. A lacy confection of a bra covered her breasts. He remembered their soft pliancy, their erotic taste and her whimpers as he'd kissed and suckled. A shiver of desire shook him to his core.

Instead of taking off her bra, she turned away, leaned against the arm of the couch and pulled off her boots and socks. He stood motionless, unable to tear his gaze from the graceful curve of her back, the gentle slope of her shoulder and the luxurious sweep of her hair as it fell forward, hiding her face.

She was undressing for him, and this time it wasn't because of an emotional meltdown. Instead of running away afterward, she'd stay. She was giving him the whole night.

The enormity of that began to sink in. He had a hunch that when dawn came, he wouldn't be ready to let her go. Yet like the birds he rescued, that's what she wanted. He'd been focused on pleasure. He hadn't factored in what it would cost him.

She faced him again and smiled. "So serious! I was hoping this would cheer you up." She unfastened the button on her pants.

"This isn't my serious face. It's my awestruck face. You're breathtaking."

"But you've already seen me naked."

"Like you said, the light was bad. I didn't fully appreciate–" He sucked in a breath when she shimmied out of her pants and laid them on the couch. "Thank you for not wanting to do this in the dark."

"I told you I was curious." Color bloomed on her cheeks. "I'd say it's time for you to satisfy my curiosity."

"Okay." His heart pounded as he threw his shirt on the couch. Once his boots and socks were off, he reached for the button on his jeans. His fingers trembled.

He'd stripped for women before. This was different. In some ways, he knew Mandy so well. In others, not at all. His first time with her had been unexpected, and at the end, awkward. Now she'd given him a chance to explore the possibilities, but there was a kicker. It couldn't lead anywhere.

If he thought about that, he'd drive himself crazy. He shoved down his jeans and briefs and kicked them aside.

She gulped. "Well, that explains it."

"Explains what?"

"Why I left your cabin so satisfied."

That pricked his ego. Size didn't matter if a guy didn't develop finesse and he prided himself on having some knowledge to go with what nature had given him. "Or maybe it was my excellent technique."

"I'm willing to believe that." She took off her bra and slipped out of her panties.

The sight of her slender body in all its glory reduced him to primitive needs. With a low groan, he moved toward her, unable to tolerate the space between them another second.

She met him halfway. The moment they touched, skin to skin, he began to shake. Pulling her in tight, he gasped at the luxury of it. "I swore I'd go slow."

"You can go slow next time." She wrapped her arms around his neck and wiggled closer as she gazed up at him. "I think we need to make some noise."

"I think you're right." When his lips met hers, it was like coming home. Even though he'd only kissed her a few times, his tongue settled in as if he'd been loving her for years. He sank to his knees and brought her with him.

Sliding both hands down her sleek back, he cupped her tight little ass. The urge to bury his cock in her warm body made him tremble. Lifting his mouth from hers, he dragged in air. "I'd better get—"

"Yes." Her voice was low and throaty.

He released her and grabbed his jeans. After he pulled a condom out and tore it open, he glanced over at the mattress.

Mandy had stretched out on it and was watching him, her gaze hot as she followed his movements. Her thighs were parted, giving him a tantalizing view of his ultimate destination.

A fresh wave of desire stole his breath. Her shyness was gone. He snapped on the condom, joined her on the mattress and moved over her. But when she grasped his hips and tried to pull him down, he resisted.

"Hey."

"Change of plans."

"I like this plan."

"I think you'll like the new one, too." He brushed his mouth against hers. "Turn me loose."

"It better be good, because I really want—
"

"It'll be good."

She relaxed her hold and he began a leisurely journey of discovery. He'd kissed her breasts the night before, but this time he savored the experience, nipping and licking her nipples until she quivered and gasped beneath him.

"*Zane*." She clutched his head in both hands.

"Hm?" Cradling her breast, he drew her fullness into his mouth.

"You're...driving me...crazy."

Just what he wanted. He continued to lavish attention on her breast while he slipped his hand between her thighs. Her slick heat almost made him come, but he clamped down on his response as he ramped up hers. Firm strokes quickly had her panting. Arching into his caress, she pressed her fingers into his scalp and claimed her release with a deep moan.

Sweet music. Slowly he kissed his way down her flushed skin and replaced his hand with his mouth. As he took her up again, her incoherent cries ended with a shout of triumph when she came. He'd reached his limit. Sliding up her sweat-dampened body, he thrust his aching cock deep. Oh, God. Yes.

Locked in tight, he held very still so her lingering spasms wouldn't trigger his own.

Her eyes were glazed with passion and her body trembled with each labored breath. "I've never...had two."

Pressure built in his groin, pushing him closer to the end game. "Let's go for three." He didn't know if he could hold out, but it was worth a try.

She shook her head. "Impossible."

"Let's see." He began to move with a slow, steady rhythm and she tightened around him. He smiled. "Possible." He held her gaze and watched her eyes widen. Oh, yeah, she could do this.

She grabbed his butt cheeks and began to help him, rising to meet each stroke with a tilt of her hips that would give her closer contact. He was in the zone, now. What a beautiful thing to make love with the right person.

She began to quiver.

He took his cue and increased the pace. "Come for me, Buttercup."

"You come for *me.*" She dug her fingers into his glutes.

Damned if he didn't. At the same time his control snapped, so did hers. He came in spectacular fashion and made a hell of a lot of noise. She did, too. Perfect.

13

Mandy lay in a tangled heap of sexual bliss while Zane left to take care of the condom. When he came back, he stretched out beside her without a hint of self-consciousness.

His relaxed behavior helped set the tone. Rolling to her side, she propped her head on her hand and gazed at him. "Here's my question."

"Shoot." He turned on his side and faced her.

"Since I can't imagine sex any better than that, should we quit now while we're ahead?"

He laughed, which made the corners of his eyes crinkle. They hadn't crinkled that way when he was seventeen. He had a man's face, now, and a man's body, and a man's...oh, yes, he certainly did. Even at rest his package was impressive.

"You won't get me to agree to that, not when we have an entire night ahead of us. We may never have better sex, but no two times are the same."

She smiled. "In your world, maybe. In my world...well, never mind."

"Sorry to hear that."

"On the other hand, repeating that last episode wouldn't be so bad."

"Won't happen, but I'm glad you liked it." He tucked a strand of hair behind her ear. "There's more where that came from, but first let's fuel up."

"Would you think it was crazy if we ate out on the deck? We could build a fire and make s'mores if Mom has the stuff for them." The chocolate cake had been sitting in a cold oven all day. That was probably a lost cause for dessert.

He grinned. "Sounds like fun. I'll stoke up the fire if you'll warm up the soup and open the wine."

"Deal."

He stood and held out his hand to help her up. But instead of letting her go once she was standing, he pulled her close. "I sort of hate to see you putting on clothes, though."

"Would you rather stay in here so we don't have to?"

"No, it's probably a good idea if we both get dressed." He tucked her against his hardening cock. "As you can tell, I have a one-track mind. We might never get around to dinner."

"Wow." She flattened her palms against his bare chest and gazed up at him as excitement curled in her stomach. "I'm impressed. I didn't think guys usually—"

"They don't. *I* don't. I'm kind of impressed with myself, to be honest. I thought I left those days behind me years ago."

"Maybe it's just a fluke."

"Or maybe it's you." He leaned down and gave her an open-mouthed kiss while he kneaded her bottom with talented fingers. When he let go and stepped back, he was breathing hard and ready for action.

He wasn't the only one. She gulped. "Listen, do you want—"

"Yes. But no. If you'll do me a favor and get dressed in your bedroom, I promise I'll be settled down by the time you come back."

She gathered up her clothes and left the room. No man had ever wanted her so intensely and it thrilled her down to her toes. Then again, she'd never been as fully aroused by any other man, either.

Once she'd reached her bedroom, she considered other options besides putting her clothes back on. He'd laugh at her flannel rubber ducky PJs, but he'd appreciate how easily they came off after they finished dinner. She put on her red velvet slippers, brushed the tangles out of her hair, and went back to the living room.

He wasn't there, but she could see him through the picture window. He'd turned on the floods so he could build a fire. In his sheepskin jacket, jeans, boots and Stetson, he was the epitome of a rugged cowboy, especially carrying an armload of firewood he'd taken from the bin under the deck.

He must have become aware of her watching him because he looked up. Sure enough, he laughed when he spotted her dressed in rubber ducky flannel. Then his laughter faded and he just looked at her, as if memorizing the image.

Logically, he'd want her to stay in Montana. He'd mentioned it before when they'd talked about training Licorice, but it had been an offhand remark. Or maybe not so offhand.

Giving her a quick smile, he went back to his work and she walked into the kitchen to warm up their dinner.

She couldn't stay. Being wanted made her feel warm and cozy, but sad, too. Naturally if she returned here to live, her mother wouldn't leave and he'd be happy about that. But her mother wasn't the main reason he'd want her to stay, not after the past two days.

Eagles Nest had become a symbol of her lost innocence, though, and she couldn't get past that. Her mother had been the only reason to visit. She was attempting to change that dynamic.

Discovering a new relationship with an old friend was exciting, but Zane was anchored to a place she wanted to forget. She wouldn't forget him, though. She hadn't been able to even before he'd given her the most passionate moments of her life. But he wasn't enough reason to move back.

She had the soup kettle on the stove, the wine open and was slicing a loaf of bread from the Eagles Nest Bakery when Zane came into the kitchen bringing the scent of wood smoke and pine trees.

Laying his hat on the counter, he looped an arm over her shoulder and leaned down to nuzzle the side of her neck. "Love the outfit."

"Me, too."

"I see you're still partial to anything yellow."

"Yep, including butter. I'm planning to toast the bread and butter it."

"Yum. Nothing like warm melted butter on fresh bread." He lifted her hair and nibbled on her ear. "I take that back. Some things are way better." He slipped his hand under the hem of her top and fondled her breasts.

"You're taking a big chance fooling with a woman who's working with a sharp knife."

"Then let me have the knife." He took it from her and laid it on the counter before turning her to face him. "Those PJs are sexy as hell."

"No, they're not."

"On you they are." He slid his hands to the small of her back and under the elastic waistband. "Just think of what I could accomplish while the soup's heating."

She caught his wrists and held on. "The soup's already bubbling. I'm tempted to let it boil over, but that would make a huge mess."

He held her gaze. "Totally worth it."

"We'd waste my mom's soup."

"You got me there." He sighed and released her. "Aunt Jo makes awesome veggie soup. Go get your jacket while I toast the bread. It's cold out there."

"I know." She backed out of the kitchen. "That's what makes it fun." She hadn't felt this sense of adventure for years.

Zane hadn't finished toasting and buttering the bread when she came back wearing her jacket, so she checked in the pantry for marshmallows, graham crackers and chocolate bars. "We're in luck!" She came out with all three. "S'mores are happening!"

"Got forks to toast the marshmallows with or do I need to bend some coat hangers?"

"We used to have some. Let me look." She ducked into the pantry and came back with two long-handled forks.

"Those look familiar."

"We used them when we were kids. There are nine, enough for your family and mine." She paused. "I mean, when my family was three people." Those were the memories that hurt. It had all been a lie. Her dad had been carrying on with other women for years before he accidentally got someone pregnant.

His blue gaze softened. "I hope you know that us McGavins think of you and your mom as family."

"That's nice to hear." She heaved a sigh. "And I appreciate all you've done for Mom, but we can't piggyback onto your traditions. We need to establish our own. That's where a different place like New York makes sense. Clean slate."

"You mean like moving on."

"Yes, exactly."

He nodded. "I get that."

"I'm glad." Relief flooded through her. "It helps to know you understand. You obviously love Eagles Nest, but I—"

"You don't anymore."

"No." His sad expression made her sigh with regret. "Sorry."

"So am I."

"And now I've ruined the mood. Way to go, Mandy."

"You haven't ruined my mood."

"Really? You're looking pretty unhappy."

"I'm over it." He flashed her a smile. "We have dinner, dessert and logs blazing in the fire pit. You're wearing rubber ducky PJs. What more could I want?"

"Beats me." She handed him the toasting forks. "Let's get all this stuff out on the deck and start our feast."

Moments later she'd settled on a deck chair in front of the fire with a side table between her and Zane to hold their meal. She'd left the living room lights on so they wouldn't have to bother with a lantern.

"Cozy." Zane dug into his soup. "This is probably rude, but don't expect me to make pleasant conversation. My mom taught me not to talk with my mouth full and I'm starving."

"Understood. Just eat." She attacked the soup and bread as eagerly as he did.

In no time at all, he left his chair. "I'm going for seconds. Can I get you more?"

"You bet. Thanks." She handed him her bowl and leaned back to enjoy the atmosphere. Sipping her wine, she listened to the fire crackle and pop. It was the only sound. Beyond the pool of light cast by the light from the house, the forest was cloaked in darkness.

Before she'd left here ten years ago, she'd begun to actively hate the quiet of rural living, especially at night when shadows were deep. She'd welcomed the noise and twenty-four-hour illumination of the city. Returning to the evening silence of the woods on her visits to her mom had been a challenge.

That had eased over time, and tonight it didn't bother her at all, maybe because she was so relaxed. Three orgasms, a hot meal and a glass of wine could do that. It also helped that she knew Zane so well. Once she'd pushed past the awkwardness of being attracted to her best friend, she'd discovered an advantage to best-friend sex.

After tonight, she'd know Zane McGavin better than she knew anyone on the planet. There was comfort and safety in that, making the sex even better. Parting wouldn't be easy, but she didn't have to deal with that yet.

The light went out in the living room, leaving only the glow of the fire pit. She turned as the door onto the deck opened. "Can you see where you're going?"

"I'll aim for the fire. Should be fine. Without the light, it feels more like we're camping." He reached the chairs and handed her a steaming bowl.

"Thanks." She dipped out a spoonful and blew on it.

"I turned off the stove. Figured we wouldn't go for thirds."

"Not if we're leaving room for s'mores." She tested the spoonful with her tongue. Much cooler. "Do you go camping anymore?"

"Not since I took on the raptor project."

"I guess that would tie you down." She began eating her soup.

"I don't mind. Kyle would watch the birds if I asked him, but I like taking care of them. It's not a chore."

"You love your life, don't you?"

"I do. I figure you love yours, since you're still there."

"Right."

"That didn't sound like a ringing endorsement."

"I'm pretty happy."

"On a scale of one to ten?"

"About a seven most days." She glanced over at him. "How about you?"

He chewed and swallowed. "Usually a nine or ten. Today it was heading downhill, but it's picked up. If I leave Mom's accident out of the equation, it's a definite ten, especially beginning around sundown."

"I see." She smiled to herself.

"Finished with your soup?"

"Not yet. Getting hungry for s'mores?"

"Something like that."

"Go ahead and open the crackers and marshmallows. I'll be done in a minute."

"I'll wait for you. We should let the fire die down a little, anyway."

She ate the rest of her soup and set the empty bowl on the table between them. "All done. What did you do with the forks?"

"Left them on the railing. I think that fire's still too intense for marshmallows."

"Then why were you so eager for me to finish my soup?"

"I can't stop thinking about your rubber ducky PJs."

She was glad she'd worn them. "Is that why you turned out the living room light? You wanted to fool around?" Her body tuned up right on schedule.

"Would you have an objection?"

"No, but I'm not sure where—"

"My chair's roomy."

"But it's hard." She giggled. "Don't say it."

"Just so you're thinking it."

"I'll be right over." She pushed herself to her feet and edged around the small table to stand in front of him. "What now?"

"Slide out of those rubber ducky bottoms."

"My legs will get cold." She was shivering, but not from the cold.

"I intend to warm them right up." He lifted his hips and fished a condom out of his pocket.

"You do realize this is crazy."

"Yes, ma'am, I do. I like crazy. Are you going to take your bottoms off or do you need help?"

She liked teasing him so she moved between his spread knees. "I need help."

"Glad to oblige." Grasping her hips, he pulled her closer. Then he slid both hands under the hem of her jacket and connected with the waistband of her jammies. "I'm sensing there's a tie involved in this setup."

"Maybe." She became giddy with anticipation. "I can't focus on anything but sex right now."

"I understand the problem." He found the tie and undid it. "Progress. Now we can just slide these rubber ducky bottoms down so I can locate the good stuff underneath." He shoved them to her knees. "There we go."

"Cold air. I feel cold air."

"Let's see what I can do about that." He slipped his hand between her thighs. "Open up for me, Buttercup."

"I can't. I'm hobbled."

"So you are. Lift your right leg and I'll fix the situation." He slid her foot free and the PJ bottoms dropped to the deck.

"Now I'm *really* cold." She wasn't, but playing along was fun, more fun than she'd ever had getting naked with a guy.

"I'm on it." Cupping her bottom with one hand, he fondled her with the other. He was a master at this and he stroked boldly, claiming her with his touch. "Getting any warmer?"

"A little." She gasped as he went deeper and found her G-spot. "You might want to...stay there...for a while."

"Thought so. Felt you clench."

"Mm." She concentrated on the sensation he created with the steady rhythm of his fingers. "That's good. That's very..." Without warning, she erupted in a warm, undulating climax. She grabbed his shoulders to steady herself as the waves broke over her like surf on a tropical beach.

His voice, husky with desire, penetrated her fog. "Warm, now?"

"Very."

"Then hang out right there for a sec."

"Okay." Suspended in a hazy world of sensual pleasure, she was vaguely aware of rustling and unzipping, foil tearing and latex snapping.

"Now." His strong hands guided her. "Put your knees on either side of me. That's it. There." He found her entrance with the tip of his sheathed cock. "Slide down." He sucked in a breath. "Like that. Hold still."

"I don't want to." The joy of being filled to the brim made her want to move. The rough denim of his jeans rubbed against her bottom and excited her even more.

"Please." He held her tight. "I'll come and I don't want to. Not yet."

"All right." Breathing fast, she leaned her forehead against his and realized she could do that without bumping into his Stetson. "Where's your hat?"

"Left it in the house."

"So we could do this?"

"Yep."

"I admire your careful planning."

He chuckled. "Thought you might."

"Can I move yet?"

"Almost." He dragged in air. "Okay, go for it."

"Yee-haw." With her knees braced against the chair and her hands clutching his shoulders, she rode him for all she was worth.

His response thrilled her. He gasped, choked, and swore. When he let loose with a few F-bombs, she knew he was having a *very* good time.

She came because she couldn't help it. Knowing him, he'd probably waited for her, but when he finally let loose, it was epic. She'd remember his jubilant cries for a long time.

When they finally stopped yelling, she took a deep breath and cupped his face in both hands. "Still want s'mores?"

His eyes fluttered open. "Hell, yes. Tonight, I want it all."

14

The coals were perfect for toasting marshmallows. Zane turned his slowly to make sure it was golden brown on all sides. Mandy liked to catch hers on fire and blow it out.

"It's faster." She was back in her chair and wearing her rubber ducky PJ bottoms again. "I'm already on my third and that'll only be your second."

"Faster isn't always better."

"You didn't think so a while ago."

His cock stirred. He wasn't ready for action, but he couldn't help that slight twitch when he thought of Mandy giving him a wild ride. "Okay, sometimes faster is better. But not when you're making s'mores."

"So you say." She licked marshmallow off her fingers. No, she wasn't simply licking. She was sucking.

"Are you doing that on purpose?"

"Does it bother you?"

"It shouldn't. It hasn't been that long since we...yes, it bothers me."

"I should let you do it." She glanced at him. "People eat food off each other all the time in X-rated movies."

"Put melted chocolate on yourself and I'll take you up on the offer. I don't like burned marshmallows."

"That's too bad."

"Why?"

"Yours is on fire."

"Shit!" He pulled it away from the coals and blew it out. He held the fork toward her. "Want it?"

"Sure." She quickly put a square of chocolate on a cracker, grabbed a second cracker and used the sandwich to pull off the blackened marshmallow. "This one's squishier than mine."

"Because I took the time to let the inside heat up."

She pressed the crackers together and chocolate and marshmallow oozed out the sides. "I like it." She ate around the edges so it wouldn't drip. "Want some? It doesn't taste too burnt."

"Okay."

She stretched her hand across the table. "Here, take it."

"Feed it to me." He leaned toward her. "They do that in the X-rated movies, too."

"I think we're supposed to be closer to make it sexy, but here." She moved it next to his mouth. "Take a bite."

He took a big one just to make her laugh. He chewed and swallowed it. "Not bad. Not much of a charcoal taste at all."

"Told you. But if you were in an X-rated movie, you would have moaned a little while you were eating that."

"Feed me the rest of it, then."

She held it and he nibbled and moaned as if the taste was giving him an orgasm. Funny how pretending to be sexually aroused could lead to the real thing. His jeans were getting tight again.

"That was pretty good. Now lick your lips."

He ran his tongue around his mouth and caught any stray crumbs.

"Not like that. Like a porn star."

"You'd better show me."

"Here goes." As she slowly circled her full lips with her tongue, her gaze traveled over him and came to rest on his fly.

The implication was clear and his cock got the message. But a change of venue was required for what he had in mind.

"See how that's done?"

"I sure do." He reached for the fire pit's mesh cover and set it over the dying coals. "You've given me an idea. Let's go inside."

She smiled. "Is it part of our movie?"

"Absolutely. It'll fit right in." He helped her out of her chair and took her hand as they went into the darkened living room. Instead of stopping there, he kept going and headed down the hall. A soft nightlight was shining in the bathroom. It would be just enough to see by.

"Are we going to wash up?"

"In a way. I just remembered something else they always have in those movies." He drew her into the bathroom.

"What?"

"Shower sex."

"You are so right." Grabbing his face in both of her sticky hands, she gave him a deep kiss with lots of tongue. Then she eased her mouth away from his. "I know this shower inside and out. I'll take it from here."

She wasn't kidding about putting herself in charge. She ordered him to strip while she turned on the water and adjusted the temperature. Her jacket and PJs came off fast and she pulled back the shower curtain. "After you."

He was fully erect as he stepped under the warm spray.

"Turn around."

His back to the pelting drops, he gazed down at her.

She had a washcloth in her hand. "First we get all squeaky clean. Stand still."

Like that would be possible. He managed to last about two minutes with her stroking that warm terrycloth over his body before he was in danger of coming. "Let me have that." He took it from her. "Your turn." He started with her breasts, and she arched her back with a soft whimper of delight.

But she caught his wrist when he was about to slide the washcloth between her thighs. "If you go there, I know how this will turn out." She struggled for breath. "I have a different ending in mind."

"What's that?"

"Let me show you." Placing her hands on his chest, she held his gaze as she sank to her knees in the tub. "Now I make good on the porn star promise."

Damn, did she ever. His moans echoed in the tiled enclosure as he slid his fingers through her wet hair and held on for dear life. At the end, he threw back his head and bellowed. It was that good.

He was ready to return the favor, but she talked him out of it.

"Let's dry off and go back to bed," she murmured. "I want to snuggle."

He was all about snuggling. But he grabbed his jeans on the way out of the bathroom in case snuggling turned into something more active. He offered to fetch her brush while she finished drying her hair with a towel.

When he came back, she'd lit the pressed log and had her back to it as she used the heat to help dry her hair. She'd leaned down and flipped her hair over her face to get the underside.

He was rocketed back to a wintry day when they'd gone snowmobiling and had come to her house to warm up and dry off. She'd taken the same pose then, except she'd had on sweats and a t-shirt, the pink one she'd worn yesterday, in fact.

If that afternoon stood out for her the way it did for him, he had a perfect way to test it. Putting down the brush, he sat in front of her. "Oh, my God, if it isn't the Bride of Bigfoot."

She held onto her hair so it hung over her face, parted the strands and peeked out at him. "Aaaa-ooooo!"

He smiled. "You remembered."

"Of course." She used her fingers to comb her hair back from her face. "We were so into Bigfoot. And I still say we heard him out there in the forest."

"It was Ryker trying to scare us."

"No, after we knew it was him, there was another howl."

"The wind."

"It was Bigfoot. That's my story and I'm sticking to it. Did you bring the brush?"

"Right here."

She reached for it.

He pulled it back. "Let me."

"You want to brush my hair?"

"I've wanted to since we were little. Ryker convinced me boys aren't supposed to like brushing a girl's hair."

She turned her back to him. "He's probably learned by now that big girls love to have big boys brush their hair. It's a very sensuous experience."

"So I'm told."

"Although I should warn you it makes me sleepy."

"That's okay. We can sleep if you want."

"That seems like a waste."

"I know." He stroked the brush lazily through her hair. "But it's not like you're flying out tomorrow."

"No, but...we might not be able to spend the night together again before I leave."

"Or maybe we will. There's that convenient path that leads to my cabin."

"Mm. True." She sounded drowsy. "Zane, I'm starting to fall asleep. But I don't want to."

"It'll be fine. You'll come to my cabin tomorrow night. Maybe Sunday night, too."

"I'd like that, but...make love to me once more, okay?"

"I don't know, Buttercup. You ask a lot of a guy."

"Oh. Then never mi—"

"Kidding."

"Are you sure?"

Laying down the brush, he took her by the shoulders. "Turn around and you'll see how sure I am."

She scooted to face him and glanced down. Her gaze lifted to his. "All righty, then." Flopping to her back, she waved a hand over her body. "I'm all yours."

Uh-oh. Until she'd said it, he didn't know how much he wanted her to mean it. That made him a fool, because she had no intention of sticking around, no matter how great they were together.

But he couldn't resist showing her, yet again. He fished a condom out of his jeans pocket for the third time tonight. That was a personal record, and he wasn't even counting shower sex.

He moved between her thighs. "Please don't expect anything fancy."

"You're fancy without even trying."

"Oh, I've been trying. I wanted tonight to be special."

"So that triple climax followed by sex on the deck was designed to impress me?"

"Were you impressed?" He eased into her warmth, heart pounding. This moment, when they were intimately joined, made him dizzy with gratitude.

"Yes. Extremely impressed."

"Then it was all part of my master plan."

She wrapped her legs around his and pulled him in tight. Cupping his face in both hands, she smiled sweetly. "You are so full of it, Zane McGavin. How could you have a master plan when you didn't know I would invite you over here?"

"I can create master plans on the fly."

Her gaze searched his. "I actually believe that."

"Point for my side." He rocked his hips. "But if you don't turn me loose I won't be able to satisfy your request."

"I know. I just like the feeling of being locked together. It's cool."

He looked into her eyes. How could she not see that what they had was amazing? "About as close as two people can be."

"I never thought I'd be this close to you, though."

"Never?"

"Not really. Did you?"

"Well..."

"Come on." She tightened her thigh muscles. "Give."

"Remember the night of senior prom? Outside the gym?"

"Of course."

"I was mad, but I was jealous, too."

"Really?"

"Yes. That idiot was touching you the way I'd secretly wanted to."

"You were jealous?"

"You sound surprised."

"I am surprised. We were just friends."

"That's what I told myself whenever I looked at you." He leaned down and brushed his lips over hers. "I wasn't supposed to feel that churning in the pit of my stomach. You were Mandy, Buttercup, the person I'd known forever. Thinking of you that way seemed wrong. But I did, anyway."

She sucked in a breath. "Why didn't you ever tell me?"

"I might have after that scene outside the gym. I broke up with the girl I was going with right after that because I knew you were more important than she was. But before I could decide whether to say anything or do anything, you left."

"I had to."

"I know." He focused on her eyes. "But I'm telling you now, because...maybe it's important."

She gripped his shoulders as she met his gaze. "It is important."

"Mandy—"

"But it doesn't...it doesn't change anything."

Damn it, he'd been afraid of that. "Right." He swallowed his disappointment. He had her in his arms tonight, which was more than he'd ever expected. Kissing her gently, he vowed to be grateful. "Now turn me loose," he murmured against her mouth, "so I can continue with my master plan."

When she relaxed her thighs, he slid both hands under her hips. Then he lifted her so he could catch her sweet spot with each thrust. If pleasure was all he could give her, then he'd learn to accept it.

15

The scent of coffee woke Mandy at dawn. She was snuggled into a warm cocoon of blankets, but Zane must have managed to get up without waking her. She heard the soft thump of the refrigerator door close but otherwise the house was silent.

Sliding off the mattress, she stood. The house was chilly because her mom had the thermostat programmed and the heat hadn't kicked on yet. She grabbed one of the blankets and wrapped up in it.

When she glanced out to the deck where they'd left their dishes the night before, they were gone. She must have been sound asleep if she hadn't heard him cleaning up.

She found him fully dressed standing in front of the kitchen counter. A jar of peanut butter, a jar of strawberry jam and the bread from last night explained the sandwich he was eating. A cup of steaming coffee sat on the counter beside him.

"Looks good." And she wasn't only talking about the sandwich. A girl could get used to waking up to a broad-shouldered cowboy in her kitchen.

He turned, still chewing. Then he swallowed. "Mornin', Buttercup." A shadow of a beard darkened his chin and his hair was mussed from sleep. The cowlick he usually tamed was sticking up.

The cowlick reminded her of the boy she used to know, but the rest of him was all man. Looking at him sent little arrows of sensation to her lady parts. "Good morning to you."

Putting down the sandwich, he walked over and drew her into his arms. "I was trying not to wake you."

"Then you must be stealthy, considering you've cleaned up our dinner dishes and I didn't hear a thing."

"I closed the kitchen door while I did that. It wasn't fair to leave you with the mess." He leaned down and gave her a soft kiss. "But I have to go in a bit. The critters need breakfast."

"And you'll be on your own again." She gave him a quick return kiss and wiggled out of his arms. "I'm going with you."

"Hey, you don't have to."

"I know. I want to. Finish your sandwich and coffee while I throw on some clothes."

"At least have some coffee before we leave."

"No need. There are a couple of travel mugs in the cupboard over the stove. We can take it with us."

"Want a sandwich?"

"I'd love it. I'll be ready in no time!" Dashing out of the kitchen and back to her bedroom, she put on the jeans and boots her mom had loaned her, another of her teenage-era shirts and a jacket. She'd left her hat on the hall tree.

She was on her way there when the mattress came sliding toward her with Zane pushing from behind.

"Didn't want to leave this in the living room. With the Whine and Cheese ladies in the neighborhood, no telling who will stop by here today."

"Good thinking." She grabbed the end and guided it through her bedroom door. "I'll get the covers." She brought them in as he was adjusting the mattress on the box spring. She dumped the bedding on top in a heap. "That'll do. We don't have to make the bed. Let's go." She ushered him out and closed the door behind her.

When she turned around he was facing her, blocking her way. "Did I forget something?"

"No, I did." He swept her into his arms and gave her a deep kiss flavored with coffee and peanut butter.

She gripped his shoulders and hung on as the explosive passion she'd enjoyed last night ignited with breathtaking speed. Backing her against the wall, he nudged her thighs apart and thrust his hips forward with a groan of frustration.

Need spiraled through her. Maybe...if they hurried...no, too crazy.

He lifted his mouth and gulped for air. "Promise you'll come by the cabin tonight."

"I will." She struggled to breathe. "I promise."

"Thank you." Chest heaving, he moved back. "That'll get me through the day."

"Or make it seem longer."

He gave her a wry grin. "That, too. Come on. Let's go feed us some critters."

Moments later she was in his truck with travel mugs in the cup holders. She didn't trust herself to drink coffee on the dirt road leading out because of the ruts, so she ate her first bite of the PB and J he'd made for her. "Best. Sandwich. Ever."

He laughed. "When it comes to PB and J, I have skills."

"You certainly do. You got the ratio exactly how I like it, fifty-fifty. Not everyone does."

"Not everyone eats as many PB and J sandwiches as I do, either."

"Wanna bet?"

"I have at least three or four a week, sometimes more if I'm busy."

"Me, too! It's easy when you don't feel like cooking just for yourself. If Mom comes to live with me, that'll likely change, though."

"If?"

"I have to be realistic. She won't want to move anywhere while Aunt Kendra's laid up."

"I doubt that'll be a factor."

She stared at him. "What do you mean? They're best friends. It'll be a factor."

"My mom would never allow her accident to stand in the way of whatever Aunt Jo needs to do. And vice versa. All they want for each other is happiness."

"Well, that's...that's great." So maybe her plans wouldn't be delayed, after all. "Do you still think my mom will be miserable in New York?"

He sighed. "I don't know. It's a tough call. I probably have no business saying one way or the other. I've seen how much Mom misses Ryker. We all do. It's no fun being far away from someone you care about."

"It's hell."

"Yeah, it is." He reached over and squeezed her hand. Then he held it the rest of the short trip to his place.

That simple gesture meant so much. He'd demonstrated compassion and understanding with that connection and she was sorry when the ride was over. The sex was great, fantastic, even, but she cherished his friendship more.

* * *

Ryker wouldn't be happy. Zane hadn't insisted that Aunt Jo needed to stay in Eagles Nest, which is what Ryker would have done. Instead he'd told Mandy that it was a tough call and now he was holding her hand instead of arguing against her plan.

But Ryker didn't have all the facts. He didn't know about Mandy's crummy excuse for a father, for one thing. And he hadn't heard the loneliness in Mandy's voice when she talked about eating PB and J sandwiches because she didn't want to bother cooking for one person.

She was hurting and Zane hated that for her. He had some ideas regarding her situation, though. What if by running away, she'd avoided dealing with any of her issues? If so, then taking her mother to New York wouldn't help.

On the other hand, Aunt Jo had stayed to battle her demons with the help of her friends. She'd moved on without leaving town. At least that was how he saw it.

But he wasn't qualified to say such things to Mandy. A couple of years ago he might have been that arrogant. Hell, a few weeks ago he might have said it.

Hearing about her dad's behavior had changed his perspective. She'd been wounded in ways he couldn't imagine, and he wanted her to have whatever she needed to heal from that. If taking her mom back to New York was that special thing, then he wouldn't try to stop her.

He reluctantly let go of her hand as the house and the barn came into view. The vehicles parked near the house were the same, but a shiny truck in midnight blue with silver pin-striping sat down by the barn. Cody was home.

Mandy sat up straighter. "Whose truck is that?"

"That fancy rig belongs to Cody. Guess he got free of that obligation, after all, which is great."

"It's wonderful. I'm sure it'll mean a lot to Aunt Kendra."

"Sure will. Since the barn's open he must be feeding the horses." He parked the truck and glanced at Mandy. "Looks like you made the big effort for nothing."

"That's okay. I'll pop in and say hi to Cody, then go check on what's happening at the house."

"Excellent. He'll be glad to see you." He reached for the door handle.

"Or maybe I shouldn't. If we show up together looking like we just crawled out of bed..."

"I'm okay with that. Are you?"

"I am, but I'm not the one he'll tease unmercifully later."

He grinned and tugged on the brim of his hat. "I can take it."

She gave him a look that would be seared into his brain forever. He would bet his last dime that in that moment, she fell for him. Somehow his cocky response had gotten to her.

It might mean nothing in the long run. She could talk herself out of being in love and fly back East on Tuesday without ever telling him. But for now, as they walked together into the barn, he felt ten feet tall.

Cody had made it about halfway down the barn aisle by the time they interrupted his work. Zane was relieved to see that his little brother had fed Licorice. That horse sorely needed a transfer to another barn, no matter what Mandy thought. She wouldn't be here to train Licorice and he didn't feel like rounding up another candidate. The mare was a lawsuit waiting to happen.

"Hey, there, bro!" Zane called out as Cody returned to the wheelbarrow for another flake of hay. "Your relief is here."

Cody paused and shoved back his hat. "Wondered when you'd decide to show up." He flashed his signature smile, the one that had been winning hearts since he'd first employed it when he'd been barely six months old. "Mandy Fielding, you're a sight for sore eyes. Come give a guy a hug!" He held out both arms. "How long's it been?"

"Ten years, and look at you! All grown up." Laughing, she wrapped her arms around him and gave him a tight squeeze. "And driving around like a celebrity in your duded-up truck."

"I know, right?" He stood back and hooked his thumbs in his belt loops. "I bought it off a friend who couldn't keep up the payments, but people see me in that truck and make assumptions. They ask if I'm famous."

"What do you say?"

"That I'm just a hard-working cowhand. They refuse to believe it, so I give 'em my autograph and they're thrilled."

"Glad you could take time from your adoring fans to pay us a visit." Zane clapped him on the shoulder. "When did you get in?"

"Around three-thirty this morning. Everybody was zonked out in the living room, so I made a bedroll on the floor next to Mom. She seemed real happy when she woke up and saw me."

"Good job. Could you get a bead on how she's doing?"

"She was hurting and a little disoriented. You know how it is. When something bad happens, you wake up and hope you dreamed it. Then you find out you didn't."

Zane sighed. "Wish I could trade places with her."

"Me, too. Deidre gave her a painkiller and she was better after it kicked in. When I left, Aunt Jo was organizing breakfast and Deidre and Christine were planning to give Mom a bath. Judy's doing laundry."

Mandy put a hand on Zane's arm. "I should get up there and see what I can do to help."

He nodded. "We'll be along soon."

"What about your birds?"

"We'll stop by the cabin before we come in for breakfast."

"Then I'll see you in a little bit." She gave his arm a squeeze and walked back down the barn aisle.

Cody didn't say anything until she'd gone through the door. Even then he kept his voice low. "I thought you were mad at her. At least that's what it sounded like when we talked on the phone yesterday."

"Well, I was, but..."

"Hey, I get it. You can't stay mad at somebody when you're in love with them."

He gazed at Cody. "Is it that obvious?"

"Hell, it's not like this is anything new. You've always been in love with her."

"No, I haven't."

"Yes, you have. Only now you've taken it to the next level. Unfortunately, I don't see it working out."

Zane massaged the back of his neck. "Nope. Not for anyone—Mandy, Aunt Jo, or any of us McGavins. I thought I could talk her out of taking Aunt Jo to New York. That's what Ryker expected me to do. But it's not that easy."

"Don't beat yourself up because you're not doing what Ryker expects. If he wanted to direct traffic he should've stayed home instead of enlisting."

That made Zane smile. "Look, you need to let it go."

"I don't want to. I'd rather be mad at him than scared shitless that he's gonna die."

"He won't. And if he'd never gone he'd always regret it."

"But he made Mom cry."

"Well, she'll be crying happy tears when he comes home in August."

Cody scowled. "He'd better come home in one piece."

"He will." Zane told himself that every day. Any other outcome was unthinkable.

16

Mandy pitched in to help her mom make breakfast while Deidre and a tall blonde named Christine helped Aunt Kendra take a bath. Judy, a petite brunette who was the fifth member of the Whine and Cheese Club, had tidied up the living room and was currently setting the table in the dining room.

Shrieks of laughter came from Aunt Kendra's bathroom. Mandy's mom shook her head and grinned. "She hates taking baths. She's strictly a shower girl."

"Don't make me come in there!" Judy called out.

"We want you to!" Deidre yelled back. "Bring your phone! We have blackmail material galore. Hey, quit splashing me, Kendra Renee!"

"No pictures," Aunt Kendra wailed.

"I didn't know her middle name was Renee." Mandy stirred the country fries while her mom put together a fruit plate. They'd also made a ginormous egg and ham casserole that was baking in the oven.

"Neither did I until I met these women. They've known each other their whole lives, so they have all the dirt, as they say. I've learned a lot about Kendra. About all of them, for that matter."

Mandy used the spatula to turn the fries. "I'll bet they've learned a lot about you, too."

"Oh, yeah." Her mom said it with a chuckle. "When the wine's flowing, we all let down our hair. Metaphorically speaking in my case. I treasure their friendship, especially since I've lost touch with everyone from my high school days."

"Me, too. Except Zane, obviously."

"A couple of your girlfriends still live in Eagles Nest if you want to call them while you're here."

She was grateful that her mom had introduced the subject of her former girlfriends instead of making a comment about Zane. "I probably won't call them. It would be almost like starting over, and what's the point? I live so far away."

The oven timer dinged and her mom turned off the heat. "True. Might as well concentrate on your friends in New York."

"Exactly. And I have some great ones. But I don't..." She paused as more shrieks came from the bathroom.

"Put that phone away!" Aunt Kendra was laughing so she must not be too upset that Judy had gone in to take pictures.

"I can't imagine any of them coming to my apartment if I broke my leg," Mandy said. "Let alone helping me take a bath."

"It takes time to build that kind of trust. You'll get there."

She wasn't so sure. Although she had a good relationship with her friends in New York, would they be a lifeline during a crisis? She wouldn't swear to it.

The people she could count on were her mom, Aunt Kendra and the McGavin brothers. Even when she'd distanced herself from her long-time neighbors, she would have come to their aid if they'd needed her and they'd do the same for her.

That left her with a dilemma. Asking her mother to leave Eagles Nest at a critical time for the McGavins wasn't helpful or neighborly. Aunt Kendra would be okay—she had her three high school buddies—but they didn't live a five-minute drive away.

Those nightly rides her mom and Aunt Kendra had enjoyed wouldn't be happening for several months, but they could still share an evening meal whenever they wanted. She turned toward her mother. "I don't think you can leave yet."

"Of course not. We haven't had breakfast."

"No, I mean for New York. I'd love for you to spend the summer there, but fall has a lot of things going for it, too, and Christmas—oh, you'll love Christmas. We'll skate at Rockefeller Center!"

Her mom smiled. "I haven't skated in years."

"It'll come right back to you."

"Do you go there all the time?"

"If you can believe it, I haven't been there yet. I was supposed to go skating with my friends this past winter but we ended up at a movie, instead. I don't know anybody who's into it. You used to skate with me a lot when I was a kid."

Her mom gazed at her with a tender light in her eyes. "That was fun, wasn't it?"

"I *loved* it. I remember the time—"

"Something smells amazing!" Cody walked into the kitchen followed by Zane. "Aunt Jo, take pity on a starving man. Tell me we're almost ready to eat."

"We're just waiting for everybody to show up. Your mom is—"

"Here! Ta-da!" Kendra balanced on her crutches just beyond the kitchen doorway. Her friends hung in the background looking pleased with themselves.

Mandy's mom nodded with approval. "Great outfit, you guys. Well done."

"And I wear it with such flair." Aunt Kendra had on purple sweats and a matching sweatshirt that said MY GLASS IS HALF FULL. BRING THE BOTTLE. With her hair in a ponytail and no makeup, she looked like a college kid who'd busted her leg skiing during spring break.

Zane and Cody moved toward her in unison, as if they intended to carry her wherever she wanted to go.

"Back off, boys." She pointed a crutch at them. "I have to learn to do for myself. But if one of you would fetch the ottoman, I'm supposed to prop up my leg every chance I get."

"I'll organize that." Zane moved carefully past her.

"We'll put her at the head of the table." Cody followed him but flashed his mom a smile as he edged by. "Looking good."

While Zane and Cody situated their mother at the table with the ottoman underneath, everybody else brought in food and coffee. The table was immense, although it didn't look as large now as it had when Mandy had been a little girl. Back then she'd believed Ryker's story that it had come from a castle in Scotland.

Eight of them fit easily even when they provided extra room at the end for Aunt Kendra and her ottoman. Zane sat on her right and Cody on her left so they could pass food to her. Mandy took the chair next to Zane and her mom sat beside her.

Deidre, Judy and Christine pretended to fight over who got to be next to Cody. He finally left the table and came back with paper torn from the pad Aunt Kendra used for shopping lists. He ripped it into three uneven strips so they could draw straws. When Deidre won, she left her chair and did a happy dance.

Aunt Kendra smiled and shook her head. "The Cody McGavin fan club is still going strong, I see." Then she glanced around the table. "I love this seating arrangement. I feel like the Queen of England."

Deidre rolled her eyes. "The royal purple outfit was a mistake. That one's on me."

"Not a mistake. I look fabulous in purple. Now, as your reigning queen, I feel obligated to say a few words."

Cody gazed longingly at the steaming casserole in the middle of the table. "How many words?"

"Just four." Tears welled in her eyes. "I love you all."

Mandy's vision blurred and she swiped at her damp cheeks.

"We love you, too, Mom." Zane's voice was gruff with emotion.

Aunt Kendra flapped her hands in front of her face and sniffed. "That's it. That's all I wanted to say. Now dive in, everybody."

The food smelled delicious but Mandy didn't have much of an appetite. Instead she was hungry for the love and laughter that flowed around the table. And jealous, oh, so jealous of the McGavins.

She remembered a time when she hadn't been jealous. Her family had been smaller than theirs, but she'd had two parents while they'd had only one. She'd even tried to talk her dad into spending more time with those fatherless boys, but he'd claimed that work kept him too busy. Oh, he'd been busy, all right. After years of being proud because she had a father, she'd become ashamed of him.

She didn't participate much in the conversation until Cody brought up Zane's raptor project.

"If you ladies haven't been to the aviary recently, you should go before you leave. It's inspiring."

"It certainly is," Mandy said. "And the pygmy owl is adorable."

"I didn't know you'd rescued a pygmy owl." Deidre's expression grew animated. "I'm for heading up there after breakfast if that works for Zane."

"You bet." Zane sounded pleased. "I also have a female golden who's almost ready to be released, so if you don't go now, you'll miss her."

"I'm hoping you'll decide to release her while I'm still here," Cody said. "I never seem to time it right."

"First I need to get Kyle to look at her and make sure she's a hundred percent. I'll give him a call today."

"Where would you let her go?" Judy sounded interested.

"Close to where I found her so she doesn't get disoriented. Her mate's here to help guide her, but I don't want her to have a long flight back on her first day. It's about a half-hour's ride from here."

Christine perked up. "By car?"

"On horseback."

"Oh." Deidre glanced at her two friends. "That lets us out."

"Now see what you're missing by not taking riding lessons?" Mandy's mom jumped into the conversation. "Really, you should all do it."

Mandy could tell from the women's laughing responses that they'd heard the pitch many times before and had rejected the idea. Their friend's accident might be the final nail in the coffin of that possibility. Which meant Aunt Kendra wouldn't have a girlfriend to go riding with her after Mandy took her mother to New York.

The meal ended soon after that and Aunt Kendra asked Mandy to walk her back over to the couch while the rest of the group started cleaning up the dishes.

"By tomorrow I'll be okay to move around by myself," she said, "but this first day I wouldn't mind having someone nearby in case I get into trouble."

"I understand." Mandy kept a close eye on her progress as they made their way into the living room. Her heart ached as she watched her struggle along when she'd been so energetic only a few days ago.

"Don't ever break your leg, Mandy." Her voice was strained as she lowered herself to the cushion.

"I'll do my best not to." She helped lift the cast onto the sofa. Then she glanced at the pitcher of water on the table next to it. "You need more water. I'll go get it."

"Hang on a minute."

Mandy paused.

"I don't want my broken leg to change your plans. I've told Jo that she can't let my accident keep her here, but I'm not sure I got through."

"Zane said you'd feel that way."

"That boy knows me well. I have no idea if Jo should move in with you or not, but my situation can't be part of the equation. I want you to understand how I feel so if she uses me as an excuse...whoops, didn't meant to say it like that. It's the meds talking."

"Do you think she's looking for an excuse not to go?"

"No. I mean, probably not. Damn, I'm messing this up." She shook her head. "I never wanted to be part of this decision and I definitely don't want my infirmity to be part of it." She gazed at Mandy. "If you can relay that to her, I'd appreciate it."

"I will. I promise."

Soon after that Zane escorted Deidre, Christine and Judy up to the aviary and Mandy went home with her mom. She didn't bring up the subject of the move to New York while on the drive. When her mom mentioned that she was exhausted and looking forward to a shower, Mandy almost postponed the discussion.

Except they needed to have it out. Either her mom was coming to New York or she wasn't. Mandy had to know.

But walking into the house where she'd shared intense lovemaking with Zane was distracting. The memories were scattered over the house like confetti. They'd made love in front of the fireplace and on the deck. They'd kissed passionately in the hallway and snuggled in the kitchen.

Her mom tossed her purse on the sofa. "You two left the place in pretty good condition."

"We, um...we tried to."

"Something's on your mind, sweetie. I can see it in your expression."

"Okay, yeah, you're right. Although we've talked about New York a lot, you've never actually said whether you'd be willing to move there. I figured Aunt Kendra's accident would affect your decision, but she doesn't want it to."

"I know. She told me."

"Mom, if you really want to stay until Aunt Kendra's better, that's fine." Mandy became aware that she was shaking and tried to hold herself still. "But if you don't want to go at all, just say so."

"Oh, Mandy." Her mother wrapped her in her arms and rocked her back and forth. "I'll move to New York. I was waiting until we'd both showered and had a moment to catch our breath."

"Really? You'll go?"

"Of course I'll go. I need a couple of weeks to tidy things up and get Zane's loan approved so he can buy this place."

"He still wants to?"

"Kendra wants him to, and we'll both work to make sure it happens. The Whine and Cheese Club will adopt his program as their designated charity. We've always thought we needed one."

Mandy stepped back and tried to sort through her mom's comments. "But you won't be here. How can you be part of the Whine and Cheese Club?"

"I talked it over with Deidre last night. I'll be a long-distance member."

"You decided last night that you'd go?"

"Not for sure."

"When did you?"

"Today, when you mentioned ice skating." Her mom's gaze was gentle. "You're right. We need to spend more time together doing stuff like that. Life's short."

Mandy swallowed the lump in her throat. "I loved that just the two of us used to go. Dad didn't like it."

"Your father didn't like a lot of things."

"Mom, I have to tell you something awful."

"Okay."

"After the divorce, when I realized he'd abandoned me for his new family, I…wished he'd died young, like Aunt Kendra's husband."

"That's not so awful, sweetie. I wished the same thing."

Mandy grabbed her in a fierce hug. "Thank you for telling me. And for going to New York." She let her go and smiled. "I promise it'll be awesome."

"I know it will. After all, you'll be there."

"We'll both be there." Energy flowed through her, washing away any misgivings. "I can't wait!"

17

Zane paced the floor of his cabin. All evening he'd resisted the urge to text Mandy and make sure she was coming. She'd promised. When they were kids, a promise had been a sacred thing, but she might have made this one in the heat of the moment only to forget it later.

No, she wouldn't forget. Not after last night. They'd bonded, damn it. She wouldn't forget the promise she'd made this morning. She'd be here.

He'd built a fire and kept it going so the cabin would be warm and cozy when she arrived. At least ten times he'd opened the refrigerator to get a beer and had changed his mind. This wasn't anything like the first time she'd knocked on his door when he hadn't been expecting her.

That had been better, in a way. He'd had a relaxing evening and then bam! She'd shown up and turned his world upside down. But now he had time to anticipate and worry about how things would go. He'd also had time to beat up on himself for worrying because in the end she'd leave, which meant nothing that happened tonight mattered. He should be more casual about it.

But then she tapped on his cabin door. To hell with being casual. She'd see right through him, anyway. Hurrying to the door, he wrenched it open.

"Mom's moving to New York!" Her voice vibrated with excitement.

He got a sick feeling in the pit of his stomach. "Great!" She seemed happy but there was a nervousness about her, too, as if she hadn't quite processed the news. He drew her into the cabin. "When?"

"Soon. She wants to make sure your loan goes through." She quickly unwound the scarf from around her neck and tossed it on his easy chair.

"Oh." That put him in a bit of a bind. He'd thought about postponing that plan until the end of the summer. He'd been positive Aunt Jo would stay until his mom was mostly recovered, and by then he'd have time to get the headquarters up and running.

"Don't look so worried. It'll work out." She pulled off her knit hat and unbuttoned her coat, her movements jerky.

"Easy for you to say." He took her hat and helped her out of her coat before laying them over the back of his chair.

"It will work out. You'll have backup." She shoved her hands in the pockets of her jeans and rocked on the balls of her feet as if needing to work off excess energy.

"What sort of backup?"

"Mom and Aunt Kendra want you to go through with it. I don't know if I'm supposed to tell you so don't say anything, but the Whine and Cheese Club is adopting you as their official charity. Isn't that great?"

"That's terrific, but—"

"I haven't spent much time around those women, but they strike me as people who get things done." She took a quick breath. "If you need funds for a capital improvement project, I think you'll have them."

"So they'll be like the Raptors Rise Auxiliary?" The mix of good and bad news unsettled him. Aunt Jo was leaving but he had a support team coming on board.

"Something like that." She continued in a rush of words. "My mom said Deidre's full of creative ideas and your mom's an excellent motivator. Christine and Judy have fundraising experience from years of PTA and Girl Scouts. You'll be in good hands."

"I'm sure that's true. I just never thought of them as a resource. I should have."

"Mom's going to consult long-distance. She'll crunch the numbers."

"Makes sense." He used to sit at Aunt Jo's dining table while she helped him with math homework. He still couldn't picture her living in New York. It made no sense to him. But she would be soon. If she'd promised Mandy, that sealed the deal.

"Hey, are you okay?"

He glanced up and realized he'd been staring at the floor. "Yeah, sure."

"I dreaded telling you." She took a deep breath and let it out slowly. "I know you'll miss her like crazy."

Reaching for her, he spanned her waist with both hands and gazed into her eyes. "An old cowboy once told me you could cure a headache by smashing your thumb with a hammer."

"I don't get it. I mean, I get it, but I'm not sure what you're saying."

"I'll definitely miss your mom. She's been a big part of my life and I can't imagine not seeing her all the time. But something special's going on with you and me and I'll..." He paused to clear his throat. "I'll miss you more, Buttercup."

She didn't say anything for several seconds but she looked about ready to cry.

"Hey, that doesn't mean I'm sorry about any of it."

"Are you sure?" Her voice trembled. "Because maybe it would have been better if we'd never—"

"Easier." He drew her close. "But not better. I'll never regret making love to you, no matter how much it hurts when I have to let you go." He leaned down to kiss her, but the misery in her eyes made him hesitate. "But that's just me talking. You promised to show up tonight. You didn't promise we'd make love. If you'd rather not, then—"

"I'd rather." She cupped the back of his head and drew him into a deep kiss.

With a low moan of appreciation, he savored her lush mouth. The erotic dance of her tongue, lazy and sensuous against his, nearly made him come. He clamped down on that urge. Mandy was a feast for the senses and he intended to draw out the intense pleasure of loving her.

Slowly he peeled off her clothes, pausing to nibble and kiss whenever he uncovered a new expanse of satin skin. But inevitably he reached the challenge of her boots. Scooping her up in his arms, he carried her to the bed and settled her on the edge of it so he could drop to his knees and pull them off.

"I love it when you do that."

Her husky comment fired his blood. "Do what?"

"Pick me up like I'm a feather."

"You're more like whipped cream." He set the boots aside and eliminated her jeans and panties in one smooth motion. "Light and sweet on the tongue." Still on his knees, he grasped her hips, scooted her closer to the edge of the mattress and moved between her thighs. Then he lifted his gaze to hers. "Do you love it when I do this?"

She trembled. "Lord help me, I do. But you're spoiling me."

"Good." And he settled in.

* * *

With a soft moan of surrender, Mandy gave herself to the incredible pleasure of being loved by Zane. He was spoiling her, all right, spoiling her for any other man. He knew exactly how to...yes, like that...like *that.* Clutching his head, she cried out as a climax rolled through her with waves of sensation that left her limp and gasping.

She offered no resistance when he gently drew back the covers and guided her beneath the cool sheets. Dazed, she lay very still and watched him undress. Firelight danced over his muscular torso as he sat in his chair to take off his boots.

The potent image would stay with her forever—Zane, shirtless in his worn easy chair, pulling off his boots so he could make love to her. She didn't know why she found that so touching. It just was.

Then he stripped off his jeans and briefs. That arousing sight affected her in a totally different way. The proud jut of his cock sent the beat of jungle drums through her entire body, but the rhythm was most insistent in the moist recesses that would soon receive all that bounty.

He made quick work of rolling on the condom and he was there, the mattress dipping under his weight as he slipped under the covers and gathered her close. She felt dainty and delicate nestled against his solid bulk, but when he began stroking her with his big hands, her earthy Amazon emerged.

She pressed her palm against his broad chest. "Lie back."

His mouth brushed hers. "Feeling the urge to be in charge?"

"Yes."

"Sounds like fun." He stretched out beside her and turned his head in her direction. "Your move."

"Hold still."

"I'll do my best."

Straddling him, she flattened her palms on his chest and gazed into his eyes as she slowly lowered her hips, taking his sheathed cock deep.

His blue eyes darkened to navy and his chest heaved as he sucked in air. "Sorry." His voice rasped in the silence. "But you get to me."

"You get to me, too." Her heart hammered in reaction to the intense connection they'd created, that *she'd* created. He'd done nothing to initiate their joining and that made it more significant to her. She'd chosen to be linked with him in this intimate way.

He swallowed. "I could come just by looking into your eyes."

"Same here." She pressed her hands against his chest. "I can feel your heart pounding."

"Is yours?"

"Put your hand there and find out."

He placed it gently over her heart. "Going pretty fast."

Taking a quick breath, she began to move. Not a lot, but she didn't need much. She figured he didn't, either. Holding his gaze, she kept up a gentle rhythm.

His fingers tightened over her breast. "Your heart's going faster."

"Yours, too."

"I can feel you squeezing...my cock."

"Because I'm almost there."

He gulped for air. "Me...too. I can't wait."

"*Now.*" She shoved her hips down at the same moment he yelled and thrust up. Her vision blurred as a powerful orgasm rocketed through her. She could no longer see him clearly but he was there in every cell of her body as she shuddered and cried out his name.

When she could focus again, she discovered he looked as shell-shocked as she felt. She took a shaky breath. "I don't know what that was, but I've never come like that."

"I thought I was dying." He reached up and stroked her cheek. "But what a way to go."

"No kidding." When she braced herself on her outstretched arms, they began to shake from weariness. "I'm...I'm wiped out."

"I hate admitting it, but so am I." He hesitated. "Do you want me to take you home?"

"Not really. I might not be much fun if I stay, though."

"You'll be all the fun I need, Buttercup, just by being here. Let me get rid of the condom and we'll snuggle and sleep. I'll set my phone so we'll wake up in time for me to drive you back."

"Sounds perfect."

After he left the bed she missed his warmth. But moments later she was comforted as she listened to him moving around the cabin shutting everything down for the night. She was safe, cared for.

He banked the fire and switched off all the lights except the one on the table beside the bed. Then he brought his phone over and sat on the side of the bed. Setting the alarm, he laid the phone down, turned off the lamp and climbed in beside her.

"Zane, it's really dark in here."

"Not completely dark." He drew her into his arms. "There's a nightlight in the bathroom."

"You don't have any security lights outside, do you?"

"No. I figure it's better for the birds if I don't have lights shining all night."

"I couldn't make my apartment in New York this dark unless I got blackout curtains for every window."

He stroked her back. "If it bothers you, I'll leave a light on."

"I kind of like the dark." Despite his gentle caresses, she was beginning to doze off. "It's like we're the only two people in the world."

"And you'd want that?"

"Mm." She nestled closer. "For a little while."

"I just remembered something."

She struggled to stay awake. "What?"

"Kyle came over. I can release the golden anytime. I thought I'd do it tomorrow."

"'kay."

"Wanna be there?"

"Sure."

"About ten in the morning?"

"Sure." She drifted in and out of sleep.

"I'll saddle Eeyore for you."

"Great." Relaxing completely, she fell asleep in his arms.

She woke with a sense of loss. The cabin was still dark and Zane's side of the bed was warm but he wasn't in it. A soft, flickering light came from the fireplace. She sat up, confused. "Zane?"

"I'm here."

She saw him, then. He sat in the easy chair wearing his jeans and a t-shirt. He must have stoked up the fire because it was burning, although not very energetically.

"Is it time to get up?"

"Not quite."

She slipped out of bed and pulled the quilt off so she could wrap up in it. Then she climbed into his lap. She didn't have to ask what was wrong. Saying he didn't regret anything was all well and good until he came up against the reality of the situation.

He put his arms around her and let out a deep sigh. "I'd hoped we could spend at least one more night together and maybe two, depending on when your plane left, but…"

Her heart ached. "It would hurt too much."

"I've never felt a connection like this before. I've been sitting here wrestling with the fact that your life is in New York and that your mom is moving there to be with you. I think I've accepted it and then I look at you sleeping in my bed, and everything in me rebels."

"Then I need to stay out of your bed."

"But that's just it. I don't want you to." He sounded desperate. "Soon you'll be gone and this is my last chance to hold you and kiss you. The world makes sense when I'm deep inside you, and I don't want to give that up until I have no choice."

"You may not want to, but it's for the best." She started to slide off his lap. "I'll just get dressed and we can—"

"Wait." His grip tightened. "Don't get dressed yet. Once more. Then we'll call it quits."

"That's not a good idea." But her resolve wasn't strong to begin with.

"You're right. It's a terrible idea. Let's do it anyway." He pushed out of the chair, taking her with him.

"You'll only make things worse."

"They couldn't get any worse."

She lost her grip on the quilt and it tumbled down to pool at her feet. She didn't bother to pick it up.

His hot gaze swept over her naked body. With a groan, he pulled her into his arms, his kiss searing her mouth, her throat, her breasts. Panting, they sank to the bunched folds of the quilt.

He cushioned her head with one hand as he laid her down and plundered her mouth. When he slipped his other hand between her thighs, she arched upward, craving his touch.

Easing away from the kiss, he trailed his moist fingers up her body and brushed them over her parted lips. "You drive me crazy." He ran his tongue over her mouth before plunging it deep inside.

The rasp of a zipper melded with the sound of their labored breathing. He bunched the quilt to temporarily support her head so he could rip open a condom and put it on. Then he cradled her head once again as he entered her with one firm thrust.

Planting her bare feet on the hardwood floor, she grasped his hips and matched his rhythm, rising to meet each rapid stroke. Her climax hovered, then swept her up, swirling her in a sparkling vortex that took her breath away.

Zane's hoarse cry came soon after and his big body shuddered against hers. She held him tight and absorbed the lingering aftershocks.

Gradually the deafening thunder of her heartbeat gave way to the soft pinging of a phone alarm. Such an ordinary sound. So at odds with the emotions crowding her chest. This was the last moment she'd hold him in her arms.

18

Zane dressed without speaking because there was nothing to say. The drive to her house was made in silence, too. But when he pulled his truck up near her front door, he remembered that he'd invited her to watch the release. He turned off the engine. "You probably don't want to come over this morning, after all."

She glanced at him. "Actually, I'd like to if I'm still welcome."

"Of course you're welcome." He met her gaze. "You always will be. Please don't shut me out like last time. I'm still your friend."

"I'm still yours, too."

His throat tightened. "Stay put. I'll help you down." He thought she might protest but she hadn't moved when he came around and opened her door. He offered his hand and she took it. Her fingers were icy even though he'd had the truck's heater going full blast.

She stepped cautiously onto the running board. She was shaking. Lifting her down, he drew her into his arms. "It'll be okay, Buttercup."

"Will it?" Her words were muffled against his chest.

"Yes. We're both strong people. We'll adjust." He had no clue how, but he'd find a way. "Come on, let's get you inside." With an arm around her waist, he tucked her against his hip as they walked toward the front steps.

"Could my mom come to the release, too?"

"Absolutely." The more people, the better.

"Then put her on Eeyore. You can give me one of the others."

"You can have Jake."

"But he's your—"

"You can have Jake."

"Okay. Thank you."

They'd reached the steps and he had no more excuse to keep his arm around her. He let her go. Damn, that was tough to do.

She turned to face him. "I'm not going to kiss you."

"Yeah, don't."

"See you at ten."

"See you then." He gave the brim of his hat a little tug and started back toward his truck.

"Thank you," she called out softly.

He turned around. "For what?"

Her voice trembled. "Everything." Then she raced up the steps. She fumbled with the key but eventually opened the door. She didn't look back as she slipped inside.

And that was that. He got into his truck and somehow magically made it home, although he didn't remember the drive at all. Instead he saw Mandy—the way her face lit up when she was happy and how she looked at him when she craved his body.

But his last image, when he'd gazed into her beautiful eyes and watched them fill with pain...that was liable to haunt him the most. He wished he could do something. Well, he could. He could leave her the hell alone.

After parking his truck up by his cabin, he went straight down to the barn. The cabin was too full of Mandy memories. He'd have to face them when he showered and changed for the eagle release, but avoiding the place for another hour or two might soften the blow.

He beat Cody down there, too, which gave him a chance to talk with Winston as he loaded up the wheelbarrow and began distributing hay flakes. "Hey, Winston," he called out. "If you think kissing her was a mistake, I can't imagine what you think of my recent activities."

The Paint's answering whinny was loud and drawn out. It ended with what Zane could only describe as a chuckle.

"I'm sure I'll laugh about it one day, too, buddy. This isn't the day."

"Isn't the day for what?" Cody came through the barn door pulling on his work gloves. "Have you changed your mind about the release?"

"No. She's ready. We're still heading out around ten."

"Excellent." Cody picked up a flake of hay and carried it into a stall. "Is Mandy going with us?"

"Yep." He ignored the sharp pain in his heart. "She wants to bring her mom, after all, so I'll put Mandy on Jake and let Aunt Jo have Eeyore."

"Do you want Winston, then? I'm okay with one of the others."

"Nah, you love that flashy horse and you don't get to ride him much. I'll take Strawberry." He moved the wheelbarrow a little further down the aisle. "FYI, it's definite. Aunt Jo's relocating to New York. She'll leave soon, maybe in a couple of weeks."

Cody stopped in mid-motion and stared at the hay flake he held. "Damn."

"Yeah."

Glancing up, Cody nodded. "That explains why you look like you were dragged through a knothole backwards."

"I'll clean up before I see Mom."

Cody sighed and went back to work. "This won't be good news for her. Wasn't there some talk about Aunt Jo staying until Mom got on her feet?"

"Mom told her not to do it on her account."

"Well, there you go. That's our mother through and through. This morning she was talking about renting a wheelchair, so she can wheel herself down here and help with the feeding."

Zane responded with a few pithy swear words.

"I know, but she's going to be miserable if she has to sit around all day. She went online last night to research how handicapped people work with horses. She's already decided lessons are doable. She can teach from a wheelchair."

"I suppose she can if she'll keep the hell out of the arena." He finished up one side of the barn and started down the other. "I could build ramps so she could get down here, but going back would be a challenge."

"She plans to develop Wonder Woman biceps to handle that part. She claims by fall she'll be strong enough to beat you at arm wrestling."

He smiled. "She can beat me, now. I'm not going to smash my mother's fist into the table."

Cody carried the last flake of hay into Licorice's stall. "You gonna send this mare packing?"

"That's the plan."

"If she responds better to women, then you could consider hiring a woman to help out around here instead of looking for a guy."

"I don't like the odds of someone else getting hurt."

"I don't like the odds of this mare's future if you give her the boot. From what Mom says, her owners are clueless."

Zane blew out a breath. "Okay, I promise not to do anything yet. I'll admit I'm not in a good frame of mind to make that decision."

"It's like a double whammy, huh? Mom's accident and Aunt Jo leaving."

"Triple whammy."

"Oh?" Cody gazed at him. "Oh. Yeah. That bites, too."

"Sure does." He grabbed the wheelbarrow handles and rolled it down the barn aisle. "Listen, I really do need a shave and shower before I go talk to Mom. If you want to tell her about Aunt Jo before I get there, go right ahead."

"Sure, I can do that. You've got enough on your plate, big brother." He clapped him on the shoulder. "Just remember, it's not over 'til it's over."

"That's the thing. It's over." He stowed the wheelbarrow, gave Cody a quick tip of the hat and walked up to his cabin, dreading it every step of the way. He hadn't straightened up before he'd left with Mandy, hadn't wanted to take the time and prolong the agony.

Sure, he'd see her this morning, but they wouldn't be alone. He wouldn't touch her unless by accident. Nothing would be the same. Ever.

He took care of the birds before going inside. A male golden circled overhead and Zane gazed upward. "Today, my friend. Today."

Maybe if he focused on the eagles instead of his own sorry situation, he'd feel less like a wad of gum on the bottom of his boot. After he'd handled his bird-care chores, he took a deep breath, climbed the steps to the porch and opened the front door.

Yeah, okay. He'd secretly hoped that she'd be there waiting for him. Like in some sappy movie, she would have decided to rearrange her life so they could be together and she'd have walked the path to sit in the cabin until he returned. Talk about delusional. The place was empty.

Not really, though, because everywhere he looked she was there. The quilt lay crumpled on the floor exactly where it had been when he'd made love to her for the last time. The tangled sheets reminded him of the moment they'd connected with more intensity than he'd felt with any other woman. The pillow was dented where she'd laid her head as she'd drifted off to sleep nestled in his arms.

He couldn't leave everything like this or he'd go out of his mind. Grabbing the pillow off the bed, he walked to the open door and pitched it onto the porch. The quilt followed. Then he ripped the sheets off and tossed them out the door, too. He slammed it shut and heaved a sigh. Better.

Shaving, showering and pulling on clean clothes didn't take much time because he concentrated on each task and refused to think about Mandy. But he couldn't leave his bedding on the front porch. Tortured by her sweet scent and the aroma of sex, he stuffed the sheets and pillowcases in a laundry bag and folded the quilt.

For now, he'd put it in the closet. He left the cabin with a feeling of relief. By the time he got to the house, the aroma of coffee drew him to the kitchen where he found his mom and Cody.

His mom was stationed at the kitchen table, her leg propped on the ottoman while she sliced potatoes. A carton of eggs sat nearby along with a bowl and a whisk.

Cody arranged bacon in a frying pan. "Just in time, big brother. We could use another pot of coffee."

"I'm on it." Before he tackled the coffee, he put his arm around his mom's shoulders and leaned down to give her a quick kiss on the cheek. "How's it going this morning?"

She glanced up with a bright smile. "Fine."

He saw Ryker in her response. Her eyes told him she wasn't fine, but she didn't want to talk about either her broken leg or her best friend leaving.

Worked for him. He wasn't fond of those topics, either. "That's great to hear." He returned her smile and started making coffee.

She finished with the potatoes and handed the cutting board to Cody. "I got an email from Deidre last night." She started cracking eggs into the bowl. "She might have found us someone to help out."

"Oh?" Zane switched on the pot and turned around. "What sort of help?"

"At the stable."

Zane had trouble believing Deidre had stumbled on an experienced stable hand right when they needed one, but stranger things had happened. "Is he buying a house from her?"

"He's buying the house, but his daughter's the one looking for a job."

"Does she have experience working with horses?"

"Deidre said she does. She liked her."

Cody glanced over from the stove. "I was just telling Zane he should hire a woman." He grinned. "It could be the hand of Fate stepping in."

Despite his grim mood, Zane couldn't help smiling back. Cody had come up with that expression when he was a kid, and it had turned into a family joke. "If you're thinking about Licorice, we're not hiring a woman to please that mare."

"I agree that would be ridiculous," his mom said. She put the bowl in her lap so she could whisk the eggs. "But we need someone. What if it *is* the hand of Fate stepping in?"

Zane leaned against the counter. "Regardless of whether we end up hiring this person or someone else, we should get Licorice out of here."

"No." His mom stopped beating the eggs and looked at him.

"Mom. She's a proven liability."

"But she won't make it if you send her somewhere else."

"You don't know that."

"Yes, I do. She's a tough case. I could see some progress, but it was slow. A man won't have any luck with her and I can't think of a single woman in the area who has the training and patience to deal with that mare. Do you know of one?"

He did, but she'd be leaving the area on Tuesday. "No, I don't."

"We're keeping her here, Zane. We might have to suspend her training until I'm able to do it again, but—"

"You would get back on her?" The thought chilled him to the bone.

"Yes." Her chin firmed. "I lost focus for a second and she knew it. I won't let it happen again. Licorice is staying."

He sighed. "I can see that." He knew better than to argue when she got that gleam of determination in her eyes.

"Good." She started whisking the eggs again. "If you have no objection, I'll ask this woman to come over for an interview after lunch."

Zane shrugged. "Might as well."

"I'd like you both to be here when I talk with her and then you can take her down to the barn and evaluate her skill level. Even if she's not the right person for the job, dealing with her will give us something else to think about." She focused on Zane. "I think we could use a distraction, don't you?"

He took a deep breath. "Yes, ma'am, we sure could."

19

An eagle release was a once-in-a-lifetime experience for someone who expected to spend the rest of her days in New York. Mandy had wanted to watch one in person ever since she'd seen a video and she'd hoped the anticipation would ease her heartache whenever she interacted with Zane. So much for that theory. She'd been an emotional mess from the time they'd arrived at the ranch.

True to his word, Zane had put her on Jake. Of the four horses moving single-file down the trail, the tall bay was the steadiest. Consequently, the eagle rode in a small carrier strapped behind her saddle. Jake was used to the routine after carrying several birds of prey out to their release locations.

Mandy was honored to be the one taking the eagle, but that meant Zane had to stay close. He rode behind her most of the time but occasionally came alongside to check that the carrier was secure and the golden was quiet. Their interaction was stiff and formal, as if they were strangers.

Up ahead, Cody led the way on Winston and Mandy's mom followed on Eeyore. The two of them chatted and laughed as if oblivious to the tension between Mandy and Zane. She hoped they were. Her mother had turned into an excellent rider and looked relaxed and happy to be here.

The weather had cooperated with a bright blue sky dotted with puffy clouds. Too bad they reminded Mandy of marshmallows. Shadowed sections of the forest still had snow on the ground, but the air was scented with the loamy, rich aroma of spring. She couldn't help contrasting this landscape with her rides through Central Park, where skyscrapers and car exhaust replaced snow-capped mountains and clean air.

Zane rode up beside her, interrupting one discouraging thought only to introduce another. This broad-shouldered, sexy cowboy would continue to take these rides on a regular basis, but she and her mother would not.

She drew back on the reins so that Zane could get a better look at the carrier straps. "Everything okay?"

"Perfect." He met her gaze briefly. "Just perfect."

"You should have taken Jake."

"No, I'm glad you're on him. I just didn't think it through very well. Seems to be a habit recently." Tilting his head back, he looked up at the golden circling above them. "Wonder if he knows."

"He might." This was the most Zane had said to her all day, so she took a chance on continuing the conversation. "If they mate for life, they must have some kind of mental communication with each other."

"But she doesn't know where she's going."

"Are you sure? She's out of her cage and on a horse, like she was when you rescued her. At the very least, I think she senses something big is about to happen."

"She's right about that." He glanced up ahead. "I'm glad you brought Aunt Jo."

"Me, too. She's loving this."

"Yep." A muscle twitched in his jaw. "Okay, let's get 'er done." Touching the brim of his hat, he wheeled Strawberry around and dropped behind her as Jake moved into the ground-eating stride that had made Tennessee Walkers famous.

Riding him after being on Eeyore was like cruising down a highway in a Benz after rattling along a dirt road in a Jeep. She appreciated the horse's smooth gait, but she missed Eeyore. He'd miss her, too. He'd bumped his nose against her chest when she'd gone over to give him a hug before they'd mounted up. Cody had said he didn't do it with anyone else.

But Eeyore seemed to love her mom, too. He'd moaned with happiness when she'd scratched under his mane the way he liked it. Her mom and Eeyore were cute together and watching them had choked her up a little.

They'd almost reached the forested canyon where Zane had found the female golden tangled in twine. Mandy hadn't been on this trail in years, but she recognized the break in the trees that signaled they were nearing the edge. The drop-off was gradual, which might be a good thing for a raptor release. The eagle could soar on an updraft or fly down to the branches of a pine tree on the slope until she adjusted to being free again.

Cody and her mom reached the edge and dismounted. "Is this good?" Cody called out.

"Excellent!" Zane called back. He came alongside Jake as they joined the other two at the rim.

Mandy's mom stood holding Eeyore's reins. "I'm pumped!" She held up her phone. "Is it okay if I take a video?"

"Absolutely." Zane swung down from the saddle and turned as if planning to help Mandy.

She'd already jumped down. The less he touched her the better off they'd be. She pulled out her phone. "I'll take a video, too. That way we'll have different angles since we don't know which way she'll go."

"Sounds good," Zane said. "I've never had a video of this. Now that we'll be fundraising, it would be great to have."

Cody ground-tied Winston and walked toward Zane. "What can I do?"

"Unstrap the carrier and we'll walk it over to the edge." Zane took heavy leather gauntlets out of Jake's saddlebags and pulled them on.

Mandy glanced over at her mom. "Ready?"

"Sure am." She flashed a smile that made her look twenty years younger.

Mandy couldn't remember the last time she'd seen her mother this excited. She'd insisted that Mandy wear the western hat and boots. Then she'd decked herself out in sneakers, jeans, a fire-engine red parka and a baseball cap under the parka's hood to shade her eyes.

Now that they were here, she'd flipped back the hood and turned the cap backwards so she had an unobstructed view. She was joyous, uninhibited, totally in the moment. Happy.

"Okay, ladies," Cody said. "Zane's about to take this bird out."

Mandy gave her attention to the two cowboys hunkered down beside the carrier sitting on the ground. She switched on the video as Zane reached inside with both gloved hands. He fumbled a little as the eagle flapped wildly, but then he pulled her out by her feet.

Dangling her upside down for a split second, he launched her into the air. Mandy gasped and followed her progress with the camera lens as the eagle swooped upward. A second eagle appeared on the screen and they circled in the air, diving and gliding in what had to be a dance of joy. A jumble of emotions crowded Mandy's chest.

After a few seconds, one eagle headed toward the horizon and the other followed. Mandy had lost track of which was the male and which the female, but it didn't matter. Zane could figure it out when he reviewed the video. What mattered was that he'd reunited a mated pair and given them a chance to fly free in this wild and glorious setting.

"Woo-hoo!" Her mom shoved both fists in the air and danced in a circle. "Awesome! Loved it!" She rushed over to Zane and threw her arms around him. "Best experience *ever*."

He laughed and hugged her back. "Glad you liked it, Aunt Jo."

Her mom spun around. "Mandy! Did you see that? Did you see how they dipped and swirled in the air? They were so *happy*!"

"They sure were!" She did her best to match her mother's enthusiasm, but inside her heart was breaking. Those eagles weren't the only ones who found joy here.

Her chest was so tight she could barely breathe. Giving up a dream was no fun, no fun at all. The rest of this day would be hell, but there was only one right thing to do. And she would summon the courage to do it.

***

Zane felt as if he'd already said goodbye to Mandy early that morning in front of her mother's house. But he pretended to tell her goodbye again for appearance's sake two hours later, after they'd ridden back to the ranch and had lunch with his mom.

It was the stupidest scene he'd ever been a part of. They said their goodbyes outside the house while his mom stood in the open door on her crutches. He wished Mandy well and even gave her a hug because Cody had and not doing the same would seem pointed.

He hugged Aunt Jo with much more enthusiasm. Having her there for the release had been special. He couldn't tell how the whole thing had affected Mandy. She'd been a lot more subdued afterward, which could be the result of their screwed-up deal.

Because he refused to watch them drive away, he was almost through the front door when Cody announced that a truck was coming down the road.

"That must be Faith," his mom called from inside the house. "Right on time, too. Give her points for promptness."

"I give her points for driving a classic F150," Cody said. "That model qualifies as an antique. It's in damn fine shape, too. Love the dark green paint job."

"I don't care what she drives." Zane watched their potential employee slow down when she passed the barn, as if she might be checking it out. "I just want somebody who's good with horses."

"And people," Cody reminded him. "You need a people person for the trail rides."

"That's for sure." Zane continued to watch the truck's progress. The driver's slow speed was respectful of the property. That counted for a lot with him. "But I'm not taking a new hire on a trail ride. Whether it's her or someone else, they'll have to prove themselves in the stable before I'll trust them with a bunch of greenhorns."

"She keeps her truck nice," Cody said. "Looks freshly washed."

"That only means she ran it through the carwash in town before coming out here today."

Cody gazed at him. "You're in a very negative frame of mind."

"Yeah, I know." Zane sighed. "I should let you and Mom make this decision."

"But you're not gonna."

"No sir." He observed that the person in the truck parked it with care. He waited to see who would climb down from the cab. They'd never had another woman working around the place. He was determined to be open-minded about the possibility, though.

But when the driver got out, he wondered if there'd been some mistake.

"Doesn't look like a girl to me," Cody muttered under his breath.

"Maybe it's not her." He searched in vain for anything feminine about the person walking toward them.

The jeans, flannel shirt and denim vest didn't help. The outfit looked clean but the clothes were so baggy he couldn't make out the person's shape. The battered Stetson disguised whether the hair under it was long or short and the boots were plain brown and gender neutral.

The face, though, once he could see it clearly, made him think he might be looking at a woman, after all. No lipstick, but the features were delicate.

The visitor paused a few feet away. "Hi. I'm here to see Kendra McGavin."

The musical voice clinched it. Definitely a woman. "Then you must be Faith."

She had a friendly smile with a slight gap between her two front teeth. "That's me."

"Glad you could make it." Zane touched the brim of his hat. "I'm Zane McGavin and this is my brother Cody."

Cody lifted his hat in greeting. "Pleased to meet you, ma'am. I'll get the door for you. Mom's right inside."

The interview went well, in Zane's opinion, and Faith seemed completely at ease when he and Cody took her down to the barn and showed her around. When she drove away in her vintage truck, he turned to Cody. "She'd be great. Assuming Mom agrees, and I think she will, then we should hire her."

Cody nodded as they started back toward the house. "We absolutely should. She's perfect. And she might be a big help to Mom."

"Yeah, I thought of that. I can even see using her for the trail rides, although I'd want to give her a couple of weeks to settle in."

"She'd probably be good at it. There's something very calming about her." Cody climbed the porch steps. "It's also a plus that she's not sexy."

"It is?"

"I think so. We're talking about a female employee on a ranch with five single guys. What if one of us was attracted to her? That could get complicated."

"I suppose." Zane hadn't even considered the possibility. Only one woman held any interest for him. He was afraid it could become a permanent state of mind, too. That would truly suck.

His mom was on the phone when they walked in. She held up her hand to signal that she'd be finished in a minute.

"I'm gonna pop into the kitchen and grab a beer," Cody said. "Want one?"

"Sure, thanks. I'll bet Mom could use some lemonade." Zane settled into an easy chair facing the couch.

"Be right back."

"Of course I'll tell him." His mom sounded agitated. "He'll want to know. If you feel like coming over tonight, please do. 'Bye." She disconnected and gazed at Zane. "Mandy's left."

"Left?" He stared at her. "What do you mean?"

"She's on her way to Bozeman. She managed to snag a flight that leaves in two hours."

"Why the hell would she do that?" He'd been braced for Tuesday's departure. This news blindsided him. She couldn't be going back today. She'd only left the ranch a little while ago, for God's sake.

Cody came out of the kitchen carrying two beers and a can of lemonade, which he gave to their mom. "Mandy's gone?"

"Yep. Thanks for the lemonade. I've been on the phone with Jo ever since you took Faith down to the barn. My throat is bone dry." She drank several gulps.

"I'm confused." Zane took the beer Cody handed him and set it on the side table. "Why would she leave two days early?"

"Apparently after going on the eagle release trip she changed her mind about Jo moving back there."

"No way!" Cody plopped into the other easy chair.

Heart pounding, Zane stared at his mom. "Why?"

"She finally faced the fact that her mother loves this place and the friends she's made."

"But she also loves Mandy."

"Yes, and Jo was totally committed to the move. But after lots of tears on both sides, they agreed it would be a mistake."

Zane winced. That must have been so tough for Mandy. She'd had what she wanted in her grasp and she'd let it go.

"I'm sorry for Mandy's sake," Cody said. "But I'm glad she finally figured out that Aunt Jo belongs here. I don't understand why she had to leave early, though."

"I do." Zane dragged in a breath. "What she did took courage. Even though it was the right choice, she didn't trust herself to stick with it if she hung around."

"Oh." Cody twisted the cap off his beer. "I guess that makes sense. Hey, Mom, you're looking kind of sad. Aren't you happy that Aunt Jo's staying?"

"I am. I just feel bad for Mandy. I agree she made the right choice, but…" She glanced at Zane. "It couldn't have been easy."

"I'm sure it wasn't." He ached to hold his brave, determined Buttercup and tell her that she was amazing. Cody had been right that he'd always loved her. He needed to decide what to do about that.

20

Mandy grabbed a jar of peanut butter and another of strawberry jam and closed the refrigerator door with her hip. She'd bought a loaf of her favorite multigrain at the bakery on her way home from the subway station and she'd insta-chilled some excellent Chardonnay by sticking it in the freezer. Did she know how to create the perfect meal or what?

PB and J sandwiches reminded her of Zane, but she didn't have anything else that was easy to fix. It had been three weeks, two days and four hours since she'd last seen him. Counting the hours as well as the days and weeks was a bad sign but her brain automatically made the calculation. If she began counting the minutes, too, she'd see a shrink.

Carrying her plate and glass to the couch, she used the remote to turn on the TV. The routine was automatic, but most evenings she didn't pay attention to what was on the screen. The chatter was better than silence for helping her think and she needed to do that. She was still figuring things out.

Immediately following her hasty exit from Eagles Nest, she'd been riding high after making a grand gesture for her mom's sake. The euphoria had lasted about a week. During the next week, she'd cried every night because she'd chosen not to have her mom living with her, after all. She'd notified her friend she wouldn't be subletting his two-bedroom apartment and that had been a bad day. Without that apartment the plan was truly scrapped.

In the last week, though, she'd been able to regain the certainty she'd had that afternoon of the eagle release. Bringing her mother to New York would have been a disaster. Her mom had rebuilt her life in Montana and Mandy had expected her to tear it apart and start over.

Yet her mom would have done it. That was humbling. Her mother's love was bigger and stronger than she'd ever imagined, and accepting that had spread a healing balm over old wounds. She and her mom had talked several times on the phone since then. The conversations were more open and honest than any they'd ever had.

Resentments she'd held onto for years were melting away. Those long talks were pure gold and it turned out she didn't have to drag her mom away from Montana to have them.

She hadn't said goodbye to Eagles Nest as she'd planned, either. She got updates from her mom on Aunt Kendra's progress and had found out that a woman named Faith was working at the ranch these days. Mandy hoped Faith would take an interest in Licorice.

Zane owned her mom's house, now, and he'd helped her move into the condo. The dialogue with her mom included hearing about Zane and his progress on the raptor headquarters. He was already living there but hadn't started moving the birds.

She was hungry for news about him even though every bit of information increased her sense of loss. They were separated by a chasm of maybes and might-have-beens. She didn't know how to cross it and wasn't sure she had the courage even if someone could show her the way.

She'd finished half her sandwich and was reaching for the other half when her doorbell buzzed. Since she wasn't expecting anyone, she figured a neighbor had ordered takeout and the delivery person had the wrong apartment number.

Brushing breadcrumbs off her lap, she stood, walked to the door and checked the peephole. Then she blinked and checked it again. Not a hallucination. Zane McGavin stood in the hallway holding a small duffle bag.

She threw open the door. "What in heaven's name are you—" She didn't get to finish before he pulled her into his arms and kissed her. As his hat fell to the floor of the hallway, she sank against the familiar sheepskin coat and hung on for dear life. If this was a dream, she never wanted to wake up.

"Ooo-weee! Where can I get me one of those cowboys?"

Mandy eased out of Zane's embrace and glanced over to see her eighty-year-old neighbor

Sadie standing in the hallway holding his hat in one hand and a trash bag in the other.

"This is…" Mandy cleared her throat. "This is my best friend from back home, Zane McGavin. Zane, this is Sadie Phillips. She lives two doors down."

"Pleased to meet you, ma'am."

Sadie peered at him, her brown eyes wide behind her thick glasses. "Ditto. I've never met a real cowboy before."

"They don't all look like this," Mandy said. "He's the cream of the crop."

"I would believe that. Here's your hat, Zane McGavin. Now if you'll excuse me, I'll take this trash to the bin. Then I'm going back to my apartment so I can book a trip to Montana. I may not find anyone as cute as you, but I'll have fun lookin'!" Laughing, she hurried down the hall.

Mandy grabbed his arm. "Come inside before any more of my neighbors show up. You don't exactly blend into the landscape."

"I've noticed. I'm pretty sure I was the only one on the subway wearing a Stetson."

"You took the subway?" She closed and locked her door as she tried to imagine Zane on a New York subway. It didn't compute. "Speaking of that, how did you know where to find me?" Then it dawned on her. "My mom. And she neglected to tell me you were coming."

"Don't go blaming Aunt Jo." He dropped his duffle on the floor and laid his hat on top of it. "I asked her not to tell you. I was counting on the element of surprise."

"What for?"

"To add some drama." He glanced at the half sandwich on her plate. "Mind if I have one of those? I'll make it for myself, but I'm starving. I haven't been on a plane in a long time and I didn't realize they don't feed you anymore."

"I'll make it while you take off your coat and explain why you wanted to add drama to this visit." He'd certainly accomplished that. Every time she looked at him her pulse rate shot up. She hadn't fully grasped the fact that he was standing in her apartment, but he seemed real enough.

"I started thinking about our history and decided you've always liked a little drama in your life, provided it was the exciting kind and not the gut-wrenching kind. When we used to play like we were pioneers on the frontier, you were all for the disasters like floods and run-ins with grizzlies."

"You loved that, too!"

"Yeah, I did. You made everything more fun." He leaned on the counter that separated the kitchen from the living area and watched her making the sandwich.

His sexy self was damned distracting. Her hand trembled as she worked on the sandwich. "How's the raptor headquarters coming along?"

"It's not."

She stopped working on the sandwich to stare at him. "What's wrong?"

"I can't use the house for my headquarters, after all."

"Oh, Zane, why not? Is there a zoning problem you didn't know about?"

"No." He came around the counter. "It's a personal problem." Taking the table knife from her and laying it on the counter, he drew her into his arms. "I moved in and discovered how much I love the place exactly the way it is."

"But that's crazy! You bought it so you could expand your operation."

He shrugged as if that was of no consequence. "I'll find another way. The Whine and Cheese ladies are already on it. I still want the headquarters." He gazed into her eyes. "But I want something else a whole lot more."

Her heart ached because she could tell where this was going and it wouldn't end well. "Zane..."

"I want to be with you. Occupying the same geographical area, the same house, the same bedroom. That place is filled with memories of you, of us. I could no more turn it into a raptor headquarters than take flight like those birds I'm caring for."

She swallowed the lump of misery lodged in her throat. "It's...it's not possible. My work is here."

"I know." His voice was cheerful, as if she hadn't just shot him down. "I wondered if you might be fresh out of ideas for fixing that issue."

"There's no way to fix it."

"I wouldn't say that. You've done a lot of heavy lifting recently, so now it's my turn to be brilliant. This is the digital age. Find out if your boss will let you work remote from Montana."

"Oh!" It was an outrageous concept, but not an impossible one. She took a breath to steady herself. "I never thought of that."

"Because you didn't want to come home. But now I'm asking you to."

Aha. His timing wasn't random. "You've been talking to my mom."

"So have you. From all reports, you've been slaying dragons right and left. If any are still hanging around, we'll fight them together."

Coming from Zane McGavin, it was a solemn pledge of loyalty. He wanted to be her knight in shining armor and a girl couldn't ask for more than that. Her doubts fell away as she gazed into his eyes, blue as the Montana sky. "I love you."

"That's why I'm here. I love you, too, always have. We've loved each other since we were three years old and we'd be fools to let go of it now. Come home with me, Buttercup."

Home. She'd been searching for it for so long and it was right there where she'd left it. Where she'd left him. His words flowed over her, filling her heart with joy and hope. "I will." She looked up at him, her best friend in the world and the only man she'd ever love. "I will."

"Thank you." With a sigh of gratitude, he kissed her.

When his lips met hers, she closed the door on a past filled with uncertainty and pain and welcomed a future shining with joy and all the love she'd ever need.

Available Now!
Cody McGavin is prepared to ride off into the sunset, but before he leaves, Faith Underwood has one small request for the sexiest cowboy she's ever met – rid her of her virginity! Saddle up for A COWBOY'S HONOR, book two in the McGavin Brothers series!

*****

Cody drew in a breath. "Listen, I need to tell you that…the first time...there can be pain."

"I've heard that but I don't think it will be a problem for me," Faith said.

"Why not?"

"I've spent most of my life on a horse. I've read that constant riding can eliminate that situation. But I just thought of something. If I don't have pain, will you think I'm lying about being a virgin?"

"No, I'd never think that. You're too honest."

"I'm not, either. I told you my starter was going out when it wasn't."

He pulled her around to face him. "Let's settle this. Did you make up the story about being a virgin to get me into bed?"

"No."

"Good enough for me." He started down the road again, his hand gripping hers.

"Let me ask you something."

"Shoot."

"Yesterday you were freaked out by my request but I sense a change in your attitude."

He chuckled. "Do you, now?"

"You seem much more enthusiastic tonight. How come?"

"Maybe it took me a while to realize what a gift you're offering. All I can say is that the idea has been growing on me ever since yesterday. Being the first one is a privilege, but I'd be less than honest if I didn't admit it's a turn-on, too."

"So the books were right about that."

"I can't say. Haven't read them."

"Well, I have, and in those books, virginity is a big deal. When a man claims a virgin, it's like they're bonded for life."

"Hang on." He planted his feet in the loamy soil. "Is that what you're after? A lifetime bond?"

"No, silly. I already told you this is a temporary deal. We each have our lives set up the way we want them so why mess with that?"

He continued to study her. "But what if you find out you really like it?"

"I hope to Hannah I'll like it. This is my only shot so I want it to be good."

"That's my point. What if it's so freaking wonderful that you want to keep doing it for longer than two weeks?"

"I doubt that."

For some reason, he found that funny. "How can you be so sure?"

"Easy. Judging from all the books I've read, it's exciting the first few times, but then the story has to end because after that it gets boring. It's just wash, rinse, repeat."

He let go of her hand and held his sides because he was laughing so hard. "Wash, rinse, repeat." He gasped for air and wiped his eyes. "I hate that I'll never be able to tell anyone you said that. It's hysterical."

"Cody, you promised me that you—"

"I won't. I swear I won't, but Zane would crack up." He cleared the laughter from his throat but he still looked highly amused. "If you're so sure it gets boring, why bother at all?"

"Because I want to experience the first part, when everything's shiny and new. At least it'll be new for me. It could end up being old hat for you."

"Somehow I don't think so."

"Only because you've never done it with me, so that'll be different."

"Guaranteed."

"Anyway, from my point of view, once the mystery's gone, I'll be over it."

"Then we'd better proceed with the program so you can check it off your list." He recaptured her hand. "By the way, I have a surprise for you."

"What's that?"

"When we get around the next bend in the road, you'll see."

A minute later she gasped with delight. "Oh, Cody. That's so beautiful!" He'd swung the truck around and opened the back. Candles flickered on the ground on either side, turning the clearing into a fairyland. Soft lantern light illuminated the cozy bed she'd seen earlier today.

As she took in the romantic setting, she became aware of a sweet aroma blending with the fresh scent of rain and wet pine needles. Dazzled, she turned to him. “The candles are scented.”

“Vanilla.”

Swallowing, she gazed at him and hoped she wouldn’t tear up. “No one...no one has ever done something like this for me.”

“Then it’s about time.”

New York Times bestselling author Vicki Lewis Thompson's love affair with cowboys started with the Lone Ranger, continued through Maverick, and took a turn south of the border with Zorro. She views cowboys as the Western version of knights in shining armor, rugged men who value honor, honesty and hard work. Fortunately for her, she lives in the Arizona desert, where broad-shouldered, lean-hipped cowboys abound. Blessed with such an abundance of inspiration, she only hopes that she can do them justice.

For more information about this prolific author, visit her website and sign up for her newsletter. She loves connecting with readers.

VickiLewisThompson.com